The Judgement of a Child

Keith Salter Ford

The *Lodge Looks Back* Series

The Judgement of a Child

This is Just for You

Keith

by

K.S. Ford

Published in Great Britain in 2023

Independent Publishing Network

ISBN: 978-1-80352-467-2

Copyright © 2023 Keith Salter as K.S.Ford

The author apologises in advance for any errors or omissions and would be grateful if notified of any corrections that should be incorporated in future reprints or editions of this book.

Email: oldgills@gmail.com

All personal illustrations have been used by kind permission of their owners.

Cover design by Creative Covers.

Typeset by BookPolishers in font Georgia (Matthew Carter).

First printed in Great Britain in 2023.

For my wife, Pam, who has to forbear my long absences in the writing room.

Contents

"Out of the mouth of babes and nursing infants you have ordained strength because of your enemies, that you may silence the enemy and the avenger."

Psalm 8:2. NKJV

Chapter 1

Scapa Flow

STEPHEN LODGE ENDURED his time on HMS Alderney. After the government closed Chatham Dockyard in 1983, he knew he would be re-posted from his coastal patrol vessel, but he had not expected to be sent to join the fishery protection work out of Rosyth. And here he was a year later, and he had been on board the Alderney for ten months with hardly any Leave, and that had kept him away from his cottage home in Ashfield and his girlfriend of four years, Jessica, even over Christmas. But it was a happy ship and the captain, Lieutenant Commander Robson, was a good skipper and a fair-minded man. Stephen was due to be going on extended leave soon.

"Starboard ten. Heading one-zero-five," instructed Lieutenant Stephen Lodge. "Captain to the bridge," he called down the intercom.

The order was given on the bridge of HMS Alderney.

The Alderney sailed eastwards at eleven knots having passed through the Hoy Mouth, the western sea entrance to Orkney's Scapa Flow, expecting to turn northwards into Stromness Harbour, but they had received a distress call.

"What is it, Mr Lodge?" asked Lieutenant Commander Duncan Robson as he entered the bridge.

"Captain on the Bridge," called out Leading Seaman (LS) Andy Williamson, helmsman, who was steering the ship, using the traditional greeting. Lieutenant Commander Robson enjoyed such formality in a small vessel like the Alderney, which only had a crew of thirty-five, but quickly told the bridge crew to "Stand Easy."

"We've had a distress call, sir," explained Stephen, who was the Officer of the Watch. "Stromness will have to wait, sir. A group of divers have got into difficulty while exploring the SMS Karlsruhe wreck and have requested assistance. If we go to maximum speed, we can be there within an hour."

"Very well," replied the captain. "It's a chilly morning and early in the season for diving. What time are we looking at? 0845. It will be even colder down below, so we had better step on it. Full speed ahead, helmsman!"

"Full speed ahead it is, sir" responded LS Williamson, as he operated the telegraph to the engine room. The surge forward was almost instantaneous, but their maximum speed was only sixteen knots.

P278 HMS Alderney was returning from a two-month tour as part of the British Fishery-Protection force in the North Atlantic. She was an Island-class ship, single-screwed, with a crew complement of thirty-five and armed with a single Bofors 40 mm gun for'ard of the bridge. Shaped like a fishing boat, the Island-class patrol boats were modelled on a converted trawler, the FPV Jura. The Alderney was due to visit Stromness for a day of R & R, rest, and recreation, before passing through Scapa Flow on her way south to the Rosyth Naval Dockyard, her home base, expecting to reach there in time for Leave before Easter. However, that would have to wait.

SCAPA FLOW IS a huge natural harbour located in the heart of the Orkney Isles. It was used by the British and other Navies in the First and Second World Wars as a gathering place for their fleets, and for training crews and repairing vessels. In 1918, following the Armistice that ended World War I, seventy-four ships of the German High Seas Fleet were interned under guard in Scapa Flow and all bar skeleton crews for most of the ships were repatriated. In June 1919, believing that the Armistice was about to break down and knowing that his fleet was unable to defend itself, Rear Admiral Ludwig von Reuter ordered all the ships to be scuttled. As a result, and even after a massive salvage operation conducted between the wars, there were still seven of the largest vessels, the battleships, and light cruisers, lying as wrecks on the seabed. And these were a constant source of delight and adventure for diving clubs and individual explorers.

Passing Graemsay Island to starboard and at the same time keeping clear of the submerged sandbars that bordered the Hoy Mouth, HMS Alderney entered Hoy Sound and turned again toward their destination.

"Starboard fifteen, Mr Williamson," ordered Stephen. "Heading one-two-zero. We will do five minutes on this line and then turn south onto the heading of one-six-five."

"Aye, aye, sir," responded the helmsman. He was a very experienced, three-badge leading hand who had served in the Royal Navy for at least twelve years and had travelled the world. He especially liked the Alderney because of the old-fashioned manner of the skipper, which washed off on all the crew. Being addressed as "Mr" Williamson was just a part of that.

"We're heading for the island of Cava," explained Stephen, "the Karlsruhe wreck is just northwest of the island, and we should see the diving boat quite soon. This will take us down the Clestrain Sound. The tide's coming in and we have the current behind us, but the waters can be shallow so, watch out for sandbars and rocks."

"Aye, sir." Another thing LS Williamson liked about HMS Alderney was that the helm was on the Bridge, and he could see where he was going. Wheelhouses on the bigger vessels that Williamson had sailed on were all tucked away below decks, with no portholes and where nothing could distract the helmsman. But here, he could see the sea and the land around him and could steer himself to where they wanted to go. But rules are rules and, being the good rating that he was, he obeyed his officers' orders.

Half an hour passed. "There she blows," called Lieutenant Lodge, who had stepped off the bridge on the port side to use his binoculars, as a small diving boat slowly came into sight. The captain had stood on the starboard bridge wing since he first came up from his cabin and now called for his helmsman to go slowly ahead. Mr Robson had studied the chart laid out on the table at the back of the Bridge and determined where the wreck lay.

"Bring us to a stop, helmsman," instructed the captain. "We'll have to drop an anchor well short of the wreck site, and with the tide behind us, the ship will swing around so our stern will be facing the Calf of Cava.

"Mr Lodge? Please instruct the boat crew to prepare for launching; we'll need to go across using our whaler."

Both crew members acknowledged their instructions, and Stephen went astern to organise the boat crew. HMS Alderney carried an experienced crew, and Captain Robson had managed them into an efficient team. It was good to know that he didn't have to instruct anyone too closely now and he let them get on with their work. The ship also had two crew members onboard trained as scuba divers – the Navy still called them frogmen – so he sent an order to them to prepare for a dive. Captain Robson would go across on the boat with the divers and Lieutenant Lodge to the distressed divers' vessel. Sub-Lieutenant Jordan Scott would be left in charge, although the skipper knew that the experienced Leading Seaman Williamson would "boss" the Bridge.

THE MV ROSAMUND Queen, a small, blue-hulled fishing vessel built in 1948 sparkled in the morning sun. The wheelhouse sat forward near the bow but a later superstructure over a deck hatch was built to prevent water from getting into her living quarters down below and now provided cover for the crew and passengers. For many years she carried seal carcasses between Orkney and the Shetland Isles until one of her owners decided it was more lucrative and a lot cleaner to ferry scuba tourists from Stromness for the seven-month Scapa Flow diving season starting in April each year. She occasionally sailed during the winter months but preferred staying closer to home, fishing mostly, during the season. This was the first diving run of the year, and it was turning into a disaster.

The Rosamund, skippered by an ex-RN seafarer, Jack Milligan, brought three tourists out from Stromness early that morning to dive on the SMS Karlsruhe, a light cruiser sunk as part of the German Fleet in 1919. The tourists, all from Canada, were Peter J. Fellowes, Reg Cornall, and Dave Clements, all in their fifties to sixties and healthy. With Jack was his son Chris, his only crew member. The Rosamund Queen provided all the equipment required for a good and safe diving experience, except the individual wet suits which were tailored to fit each diver.

SMS Karlsruhe was a Königsberg-class light cruiser commissioned in 1916, but not in time to participate in the Battle of Jutland between the British Grand Fleet and the Germans when neither side won a decisive victory and over six thousand British lives were lost. The battle confirmed British naval dominance and secured control of the shipping lanes, blockading the German High Seas Fleet, but the Karlsruhe saw action, particularly against the Russian Fleet before she was sunk at Scapa. She lay in shallower waters than many of the Scapa wrecks, eighty-two feet deep, which allowed for a longer diving experience of about forty minutes duration, popular with novice scuba divers. Although the ship lay heavily on the silted seabed, her port side was exposed and enabled divers simply to view the wreck through the many holes that war damage, rust, and salvaging, had made in the hull.

HMS ALDERNEY ANCHORED about a nautical mile from Rosamund Queen and, as the skipper had predicted, swung around on the tide until her stern pointed to the northern tip of Cava Island, the Calf. The Karlsruhe wreck site was less than a mile offshore from the island in clear waters. The Alderney's whaler was lowered by its gantry, and the Royal Navy crew set off. As she approached the dive boat, the whaler's coxswain, an Able Seaman named Joe Hall cut the outboard motor, and drifted alongside the Rosamund, throwing a rope over a cleat, and securing the whaler. Jack Milligan greeted Lieutenant Commander Robson as he clambered aboard. The seas were light, and the day was crisp and cold but sunny. On the diving boat were Jack's twenty-year-old son Chris and one other middle-aged man, who was introduced as one of the Canadian scuba tourists, Dave Clements.

"What's happened here then?" the captain inquired.

Jack Milligan responded, "I have two missing divers down below. They and Mr Clements here dived at about seven o'clock this morning and only Mr Clements made it back to the boat."

"But it's nearly 10:00 now." Stephen Lodge was instantly concerned. "How much air would they have and is there a chance of their survival now?"

"No, not if they're down below," a distressed Jack Milligan spluttered, "We use twelve litre steel bottles, two per diver, and each bottle gives a good hour's dive time although a single dive should not last longer than forty minutes. Mr Clements here took longer before he surfaced because, he said, he was looking for his colleagues after they got separated exploring the hull."

"And Mr Clements," Captain Robson addressed the man who was still in his wetsuit, sat crumpled on a thwart with his head in his hands. "Tell us about your dive, please?"

Dave Clements looked up, red-faced and tearful, "I came over from Canada with my friends, Peter, and Reg to try scuba-diving in the Scapa Flow. We're not very experienced divers, but we've done a bit of coastal work around Newfoundland Island, where we all have businesses and families. Today was our first dive.

"Anyway," he continued, "we all went down this morning and swam around the hull of the wreck. Jack and Chris recommended the Karlsruhe because it's shallow, so we would have a longer dive, and the water is clear. We had a good look around, saw the anchors lying in the silt at the bow, and examined the Bridge section, what the brochure calls the Armoured Control Tower.

"I'm not as experienced as Pete and Reg, so I did not want to swim inside the wreck, but the exposed boiler room was too tempting for them. I left them to it while I went back to look at the capstans on the fo'c'sle. And that was the last I saw of them. I spent some time studying the capstan mechanism – we're all engineers back home – and when I realised my air was running low, I came up to the surface. That's what we had agreed, to make our own way back when we'd seen enough."

"Your air was running low?" asked Stephen, "I

thought you had enough air for a full hour; had you been down that long?"

"No," replied Dave Clements, "I had only been down for about forty minutes. We planned on two dives today with a rest break in between and had a second bottle each on board. I was surprised to find my air was so low on that first dive."

"Mr Milligan?" the captain said, addressing Jack. "I thought you'd said all divers were given enough air for two hours?"

Jack Milligan, the skipper of the dive boat bristled. "If they took both bottles with them but we wouldn't recommend a single dive to go much over the hour for the less experienced. We filled the bottles overnight and checked them all onboard this morning. All three gentlemen checked their own bottles before they dived. They were all good for one hour per bottle, but every diver breathes at a different rate."

"And that was why I was surprised to find I was so low!" explained Dave Clements. "I had checked my own bottles when I first came aboard, and they were fine. Jack and Chris had set them up as agreed."

"Well, this isn't getting us nearer to finding the other two." Captain Robson gave instructions to his divers, who were still on the ship's whaler, to tool up and drop into the water. "Make sure you check all your equipment before you go down. I know you familiarised yourselves with a map of the wreck before we came across so go direct to the boiler room and start your search there."

"Aye, sir," said John (Dinger) Bell, the leader of the two-man Alderney diving team. We'll be as quick as we can."

The two ratings, already in their wet suits, put their scuba equipment on and made sure everything was working. They dipped their masks overboard in the water to prep the temperature of the glass lens and provide a better seal, and then both men rolled backwards into the water. They were gone within minutes.

"Is it possible there was a fault with the air gauge?" asked Stephen of the dive boat's skipper. "Could there have been a fault with all of them?"

"They were working fine this morning," Chris Milligan joined the conversation. "I balanced the bottle gauges, all of them, with the main compressed air tank gauge and they were all agreed on the amount of air pumped into the bottles."

"So, when you put the first bottle on before your dive," Stephen was now addressing Dave Clements, "you rechecked the gauge?"

"No," said Dave. "Like I said, I'd already done that when I first came aboard so I didn't need to do it again."

"And was the bottle turned on when you placed the mask over your face?"

"Of course, it was," responded Dave, surprised by the question. "How would I breathe otherwise. But I had only just turned it on."

"Could it have already been turned on? Just

slightly? Enough to drain a small amount of air over a period and you wouldn't have noticed." Stephen was pursuing a line of reasoning that no one other than the captain was recognising.

"We'd have heard it," said the skipper, Jack Milligan.

"Where were the bottles being kept?" pushed Stephen.

"Under the thwarts," said Chris, "with the rest of their gear."

"Back packs, coats, and everything," Stephen was sure now. "So, if the tanks were lying under all the other paraphernalia, you might not have heard the air escaping!"

"That's possible I suppose," said Jack defensively, "but we'd have known when the divers got their kit on."

"Except, you wouldn't," said Stephen finally, "because Mr Clements did not recheck his bottles, and I would guess all three men helped each other to mount their equipment?"

"You are correct," Dave Clements had caught on to what Stephen was implying. "Reg put mine on, and I did Peter's."

"And who checked Reg?"

"He did his own," said Dave. "He's got more experience than us two."

"Well, let's see what the divers have got for us," the captain interrupted Stephen's line of questioning. He had seen the divers' marker buoy bob up and down three times, a Navy-trained signal that at least one of the divers was ascending to the surface.

DINGER BELL BROKE the surface just close to the Rosamund Queen and swam to the side. Holding on to a fender he removed his mask and spoke to Captain Robson.

"We've found one of the men, skipper," Dinger spoke despondently, "but he's a goner. Caught up on a part of the superstructure inside the boiler room. Looks like his airline got snagged!"

"What about the other man?" asked the captain.

"Nowhere to be seen, sir. Not in the boiler room."

"Have you looked anywhere else? You had best go right around the hull and have a good explore."

"Sid needs a hand getting the body up first, sir."

"No," the captain was adamant, "Leave it there, we can't do any good now. Search and Rescue will be right behind us, and the RNLI can take over the investigation. I don't like what I'm hearing, and we need to find that other man, that other body I suppose, before we can reach any conclusions."

Dinger Bell, so called in the tradition of the Navy, put his mask back on and dived. He went back to his mate, Sidney Saunders, and signalled him to follow as they looked around the rest of the wreck, taking their time and paying close attention to any nooks and crannies as they did so. It wasn't long before they found a discarded air tank on the seabed, but no body. They were running out of air themselves so the pair of them returned to the Rosamund just as the RNLI lifeboat arrived. The air tank was hoisted on board by Chris Milligan, and the RNLI dropped their own divers overboard to recover the body that the two sailors had found.

THE INVESTIGATION TOOK several hours. One of the voluntary lifeboatmen was also a Stromness police officer and he cautioned the crew of the Rosamund Queen and the scuba-tourist Dave Clements, that further questions would need to be asked, "but these are just routine." The body was brought to the surface and identified by Dave as that of his friend, Peter J Fellowes, his bloated face disfiguring the fifty-five-year-old man, but still recognisable. There was no sign of Reg Cornall, but the empty air tank was identified as one that he had used.

"Take a look at this, Captain," one of the lifeboatmen spoke to Lieutenant Commander Robson. "Look at his air hose connecting the regulator to the pressure gauge. There is a faint tear in the rubber, too uniform to be a snag. More like a cut from a very sharp knife. Small enough not to be seen unless you are looking for it but big enough to let the air out and drown the diver."

"So, this could be deliberate?" Stephen was alert, looking at Mr Fellowes diving equipment himself now. "And if it is, could this be done before the dive started?"

"No, sir," the RNLI man was certain. "The air

loss would have been too quick not to have noticed straightaway."

"So, this would have had to occur after the dead man and Mr Cornall had separated from Mr Clements here."

"Yes, sir," the RNLI man responded, "Mr Fellowes would have been dead within two minutes unless he could get to the surface quickly, and the way we found him on that superstructure would have prevented him from doing that."

"Are you saying what I'm thinking?" the captain asked.

"Yes, sir. Mr Fellowes was hitched up unusually high, and the way he faced forward was odd. There was no way he could snag his own air tubes, they are designed to be compact with the wetsuit, but he was too caught up to get down without help. If his airway was cut, he may have been placed in that position by the other diver."

"And that makes Mr Cornall our chief suspect," said the captain.

"Yes, sir," the RNLI man concluded.

"And we need to find him," the captain told Stephen. "We'll have to run the whaler around the wreck site, and across to Cava if we have to, but we can't leave the scene until we know Mr Cornall is no longer in the water."

BUT THEY DID not find Reg Cornall until mid-afternoon. His body had been swept by the incoming tide toward the island of Cava and was washed up on a beach. There are very few residents on the island, farmers mostly, and one of those was out walking their dog when they spotted the body just as HMS Alderney's whaler came into view. Under instruction from the Captain, Dinger Bell and Sidney Saunders waded ashore and retrieved the body so they could take it back to the Rosamund Queen.

"Where's his scuba equipment, Dinger," asked Stephen as they reached the boat.

"He had nothing with him when he was found, sir," replied the diver, "and there's no evidence on the sand flats going in."

"So, it looks like he offloaded all his kit and tried to swim ashore to get away from the scene of crime, so to speak!"

"I'm not so sure," Captain Robson said, briefly examining the body. "Look at the size of him, barely five feet tall and very slight, and older than Mr Fellowes I would say. And he, Mr Fellowes, is nearer six feet and overweight."

"Being in water displaces weight, sir," said Stephen, "and we all know what it's like when you lift the wife or girlfriend in the swimming pool."

"Speak for yourself, Mr Lodge," the captain retorted. "But I know what you're saying. No, there's something going on here and it doesn't quite add up. We'd best get Mr Cornall's body back to the dive boat and get the RNLI to give him a once over. I know they've got a doctor with them."

Chapter 2

The Inquest

MR CORNALL'S BODY was ferried on the ship's whaler back to the Rosamund Queen where Dave Clements formally and swiftly identified him. The RNLI lifeboat took the diving boat in tow, and with HMS Alderney as escort, returned to Stromness, where a provisional post-mortem was quickly conducted on both bodies.

Mr Cornall, it was decided, had died of a heart attack caused by over-exertion while on the dive. He had a little water in the lungs but had not drowned, unlike Mr Fellowes who had asphyxiated due to a lack of oxygen and whose lungs had a quantity of water. The small cut in his airway would have caused him to drown within five minutes by letting water in when his air had escaped.

A coroner's inquest was to be set up within two days and the ship's officers of HMS Alderney were requested to attend along with the RNLI investigative team. Stephen cursed his luck because it meant a delay to the start of his Leave but accepted the necessity for it. Conversely, the ship's crew were happy to have a couple of days extra in port after two months floating around the North Atlantic.

Dave Clements, who had been staying at the Stromness Hotel near the harbour was asked to remain there until the inquest, while Jack Milligan's boat was seized for forensic examination and Jack and his son, Chris, being Stromness residents, were confined to home.

ON THE DAY of the inquest, the two Royal Navy divers gave evidence to where they had found Peter Fellowes and the body of Reg Cornall, and where they had picked up the air tank belonging to Mr Cornall. The RNLI divers told how they had found Mr Fellowes caught up on the boiler room superstructure and explained the unusual nature of his position. They also spoke about the small nick in one airway tube that could not be the result of snagging but, in the absence of a sharp knife, could be a flaw made earlier and not spotted. Although the cut had not completely pierced the rubber on the tube, they said, this would have blown outwards under pressure from the compressed air reacting on the weakened skin of the airway. The water pressure at the depth of the dive, eight-two feet, would have contributed, and would have allowed enough water in to drown Mr Fellowes.

Jack Milligan and his son gave details of what air bottles were used and how they were set up to provide adequate air for a forty-five-minute dive with an air reserve for another twenty minutes. They were adamant that all diving equipment was checked and accepted by the three recreational divers when they first came aboard, but accepted that they, the crew, should have rechecked the bottles and gauges before the actual dive.

The coroner questioned Dave Clements about the details of his dive, and he gave the same story that he had given to the Alderney's captain, Lieutenant Commander Robson. After a few minutes deliberation, the coroner advised the court that, disregarding the flaw in the airway tube, with insufficient evidence to suggest otherwise he was inclined towards a verdict of death by misadventure for Mr Fellowes, and that Mr Cornall must have got into difficulties, perhaps because of trying to help his friend and looking for help from Mr Clements.

It was a poor verdict, and Lieutenant Commander Robson said so. The coroner, who simply wanted to get back to his day job as a General Practitioner, asked if the Navy had any further evidence to put forward and HMS Alderney's skipper requested permission to question Mr Clements. The coroner could not think of a reason to refuse the request and reluctantly agreed.

"But do remember, Captain Robson, that this is a hearing and not a trial," he warned.

"MR CLEMENTS," BEGAN the captain. "You told us that you had become separated from your friends because they wanted to investigate inside the boiler room of the Karlsruhe, and you felt it was unsafe to do so?"

"No, sir," replied Dave Clements, "I said that they were keen to examine the boiler room, but I felt that my lack of diving experience did not give me the confidence to join them."

"And so, you went back to the bow section of the wreck and looked at the capstan mechanism."

"Yes, sir. We are, we were all engineers so how things work was of common interest to us all."

"And you say," continued the captain, "that your dive lasted forty minutes due to a lack of air in your tank?"

"Yes, sir. I was surprised by that and ascended early because of it."

"Yet the boat's skipper, Mr Milligan, said that you had dived for longer while you looked for your colleagues."

"Well, yes," Dave Clements looked uncomfortable at this line of questioning. "Of course, I might have taken a bit longer but..."

"But" the captain interrupted him, "you knew where they were, in the boiler room."

"So?" queried Mr Clements.

The captain continued. "So, you knew where to look, and it would not have taken five minutes to reach your friends... but you had already agreed that you would all make your own way back to the boat when your dive was concluded?""

"Where are you going with this line of questioning,

Captain Robson?" It was the coroner's turn to interrupt proceedings.

"Well, sir," Duncan Robson explained, "the RNLI have already given evidence that suggests the dead man, Mr Fellowes, could not have got into the difficulties he did without assistance from a third person.

"And all that we've heard so far would suggest that third person to be Reg Cornall. But, when we found Mr Cornall's body on Cava, I observed that here was a man hardly five feet tall and not weighing much over ten stone, while Mr Fellowes is a good six feet and easily seventeen stone, so I couldn't see how Mr Cornall alone, could have lifted Mr Fellowes into the position he was found."

Dave Clements shuffled with discomfort on his seat.

"Yesterday," the captain continued, "I took my number one, Lieutenant Stephen Lodge, present in this court today, and my own divers on one of your other dive boats and returned to the Karlsruhe to look for the missing scuba equipment that Mr Cornall left behind when he fled the scene. We already have his air tank; that was retrieved by my divers near the bow on the day of the accident.

"We found the missing equipment tucked inside the capstan mechanism where Mr Clements said he had been looking rather than accompanying his friends inside the boiler room, and we found some alarming evidence!

"We found that Mr Cornall's equipment straps holding his air tank had been cut so that his bottle would fall free, but there was no knife on Mr Cornall's person, nor could we find one where we found his scuba equipment or his air tank. On re-inspection of the air tank itself, we found that a third of the compressed air had been used, which would suggest that Mr Cornall had taken air from the bottle for only about twenty minutes, half an hour at most given that he was a small man and had a lower lung capacity than his two larger colleagues. He was also, we are told, the more experienced diver of the three and would know how to pace himself underwater. That experience, for me, conflicted with the idea that he would overexert his efforts while on a dive."

Duncan Robson was looking at Dave Clements, but it was the coroner who spoke.

"What are you suggesting, Lieutenant Commander Robson?" asked the coroner, an elderly gentleman, with an air of frustration. He had hoped this would be a simple case of accidental death which was the usual verdict on these dives.

"Mr Clements," the captain started, "I put it to you that you did in fact go into the boiler room with Mr Fellowes and Mr Cornall, and that it was you who engineered Mr Fellowes onto that superstructure, with Mr Cornall's help, after cutting the airway tube with a diver's knife, ensuring that Mr Fellowes would die from the subsequent lack of air, and that this was a premeditated murder meant to occur as early in the dive as possible."

Everyone looked at Dave Clements expecting him to protest this accusation, but he did not. He just sat there staring at his accuser.

The captain continued. "I also put it to you, Mr Clements, that after the two of you had killed Peter Fellowes, you swam around the hull to the bow and the capstan area, where you and Mr Cornall got into a tussle over what you had just done and that, after you sliced the straps on his scuba-equipment, Mr Cornall tried to escape by swimming away but was overcome by exertion and the lack of breathing equipment."

"Mr Cornall died," concluded the captain, "not from the exertion of what had been done to Mr Fellowes, but from his efforts to swim to safety. You knew, sir!" he addressed Mr Clements directly, "that Reg Cornall had a weakened heart condition, and this would be his last dive because of it. You had planned what would happen to Mr Fellowes and gambled on Mr Cornall's accidental death, but it required you to get his air tank off him. In that struggle and his escape, Mr Cornall's heart gave way and he died. And you callously let the current sweep his body away to the island of Cava!"

Finally, Dave Clements spoke. "And how would I do that? None of us were carrying knives, so how Peter's airway got cut, or Reg's straps broke, I do not know. Like I said, I went to the bow end while they swam to the boiler room."

"Where you killed Peter Fellowes," accused Duncan Robson. "Having coerced Mr Cornall into helping you! You then had to get rid of the evidence, so you hid the knife, but not before fighting with Reg Cornall and cutting his straps. Mr Cornall tried to swim to safety, but the exertion of that swim was too great for him, and he died before being swept away by the tide toward Cava."

"But I didn't have a knife," stated the accused Mr Clements.

"No, you didn't," the captain retorted, "but Mr Fellowes did. And it was his knife that you used to cut his airway with, and very cleverly I must say to make it look as if the weakened airway had burst. And it was that knife that you used to cut Reg Cornall's breathing equipment, but you did not plan on the bottle falling loose and you could not bring the rest of the scuba equipment back to the surface as well as your own, because it would take too much explaining.

"And why would I then spend so much time underwater once I completed what you are accusing me of?" asked Dave Clements, "As you know, my air tank was nearly exhausted when I got back to the Rosamund?"

"Yes," said the captain, "it was. Not because of time spent on the dive, though, and that threw us off for a while. That was both an error on your part and the part of the boat crew. You made the mistake of telling us that you were not down for more than forty minutes, which was correct, but Mr Milligan and his son thought that it must have been longer because the gauge on your compressed air bottle suggested it. None of us thought that you might have let the air out yourself to give a different impression of the duration of your dive or that there was a problem with the tank."

"And the second mistake you made was to bring the knife back to the Rosamund Queen, where you hid it amongst the fishing and diving tackle on the boat, where the forensics team found it yesterday and brought it to me!" Duncan Robson gave his first lieutenant, Stephen Lodge, the signal to bring forward a diver's knife wrapped in a plastic evidence bag to present to the court.

"I think you will find," he said, addressing the coroner, "that David Clements fingerprints are the only ones remaining on that knife."

David Clements had slumped into his seat, looking crestfallen.

"I have heard enough," declared the coroner, "to believe that the deaths of these two gentlemen, Mr Peter J Fellowes, and Mr Reginald Cornall, have occurred in suspicious circumstances, and that Mr David Clements must be held in custody until further investigations into this tragic accident can be conducted.

"Officers," he addressed two policemen waiting at the back of the court." Please prepare to escort Mr Clements to the Station. And Lieutenant Commander

Robson? I'm not sure if I should thank you for bringing such an air of excitement to my usually dull court proceedings, but I applaud your tenacity at getting to the truth of the matter. Whatever made you suspect Mr Clements of foul play?"

Lieutenant Commander Robson smiled. "Firstly, I could not believe that Mr Cornall, being so small, had the ability to kill Mr Fellowes by himself. It is possible, sir, and sometimes necessary when you are in the Services to get answers to your questions quickly. I spent the last thirty-six hours inquiring of the Canadian Police Force on Newfoundland Island for information regarding these three men. They were indeed friends and well known on the island, but they were also business rivals. David Clements' business is the weakest of the three and he was trying to do a deal with Reg Cornall, who he knew was facing retirement due to his heart condition – included in a medical report the police sent me. Peter Fellowes was blocking the deal because the proposed Clements/Cornall merger would take business away from his own company. I don't entirely understand why Reg Cornall went along with the murder of Mr Fellowes, I'll leave that one for your own police to sort out, but I think he panicked after the event and that put Mr Clements at risk of the truth coming out."

"And the rest we seem to know," concluded the coroner. "This hearing stands adjourned, and the details will be referred to the Crown Court on the mainland." The gavel crashed down, and Dave Clements was led away.

"DOES THIS MEAN, skipper," asked Lieutenant Stephen Lodge as they left the courthouse cum town hall, "that we can go home now?"

"Yes, Mr Lodge, it does. We will leave on the afternoon tide, but I want us to pay our respects at the graveside of HMS Vanguard, so it'll be dark before we get out of the Flow, if that's all right with you."

"Of course, Captain," responded Stephen, acknowledging the obligation for all Royal Navy ships to visit the designated war grave sites of HMS Vanguard and/or HMS Royal Oak if they were passing through Scapa Flow.

HMS Vanguard, a St Vincent class battleship built in Barrow in Furness and launched in 1909, tragically sunk in Scapa Flow in 1917 with a total loss of the 843 crew when faulty cordite exploded within the vessel, and it sunk in minutes. Only two men survived the explosion.

HMS Royal Oak had seen action in World War One and during the "peaceful" years between the wars but was sunk at Scapa in October 1939. The Revenge class super-dreadnought battleship had been extensively refitted during the wars, thickening the steel superstructure, and adding weight to her displacement, but this made her slower and she was regarded by Winston Churchill, the war minister, as a "coffin ship." She was too slow to keep up with the modern convoys, but still able to pack a punch as a defensive vessel, so the Royal Oak was moored in Scapa Flow at the start of the Second World War to provide air defences against attacks on the rest of the fleet. A daring German submarine, U-47 under the command of Günther Prien, got past the primitive blockships meant to defend the narrow Kirk Sound through St Mary's Bay in the east of Scapa, and after three torpedo salvoes, sank the Royal Oak with the loss of 800 lives.

"But I have some other news for you, Lieutenant Lodge," said the captain as they walked back to their vessel. "Following a transfer request, you will be leaving us at Rosyth, and shall report to HMS Nelson, Victory Barracks in Portsmouth, at 0800 on the 10th of May, when you will be reassigned."

"A transfer request, sir?" spluttered Stephen. "But I haven't requested to leave the Alderney."

"And we shall be sorry to see you go," said Lieutenant Commander Duncan Robson. "But the transfer orders have come direct from the Ministry of Defence. You have some friends there and they think you are, and I quote, 'too far away to be readily accessible.'"

Stephen blushed as he realised who was behind this reposting. That could mean only one thing, but Stephen Lodge was determined that he would have his full Leave due before reporting anywhere.

HMS ALDERNEY DULY sailed on the p.m. tide and silently glided past the wreck of HMS Vanguard just off the north-western shore of Flotta Island, casting the usual wreaths into Scapa Flow's waters while the ship's piper played a lament on his Bosun's Pipe. In the dark, she made her way around the Calf of Flotta and through the Sound of Hoxa before turning east and south into the Pentland Firth and passing Duncansby Head to starboard. The ship was tied up in HM Dockyard, Rosyth by the start of the second dogwatch, 1800, the next day.

Chapter 3

Tripoli, Libya

STEPHEN LODGE WAS glad to get home to Ashfield. He had bought Farthing Corner House, Mrs Smith's cottage, after she died in October 1982, when it was revealed that she and Albert had bequeathed their estate to the upkeep of St Joseph's Church and the village hall. Fortunately, Jessica had also fallen in love with the property when she visited at the end of that unfortunate incident with Nikolai Volkov, when he, Volkov, had abducted little Harri Jasper. But that was water under the bridge now and Stephen had given up his rented flat in London, sharing expenses and staying with Jessica when he had to go to the city, and moved into the cottage before Christmas 1982. The money that he inherited from his parents' estate, themselves victims of Volkov's vengeful pursuit of Stephen, had adequately paid for the cottage.

Of course, some changes had to be made. The old-fashioned wallpaper had been modernised in most of the rooms, and the gas fires in the bedrooms that had caused the death of Hilda Smith when Volkov's colleague, Dmitri Mikhailov, had ruthlessly opened the gas valves with no flame, were replaced with a centrally heated radiator system, except in the sitting room where a modern real-flame gas fire was installed. Bedroom chimneys were sealed off to stop the heat escaping through them and the old fireplaces were retained and redecorated attractively. Bookshelves and bureaux were kept, as were Mrs Smith's two pairs of armchairs that adorned the windows in the sitting and living rooms. The furniture, though old, was too comfortable to be removed completely.

Jessica had modernised the kitchen as well and replaced the over-twenty-year-old washing machine in the utility room, which even Hilda had described as "cantankerous." The simple fact was that as soon as Mrs Smith had died the blasted machine would not work properly for anyone else.

Jessica cosied up the living room, removing the small dining table and replacing it in the kitchen with a folding six-seater oak table and matching chairs. She kept the serving hatch between the two rooms for late night coffees and afternoon teas to be passed through. Her mum and dad came and stayed often, helping with the work, but Jessica, who still retained the London flat for her Monday to Friday job at the Foreign and Commonwealth Office, loved to come to Ashfield at weekends and tinker around the cottage as well as soak up the country atmosphere.

There was only one job left to do and that was entirely down to Stephen. Since he had driven his dad's white Vauxhall Viva SL to the cottage, it had been kept on the driveway under the grey-green tarpaulin used to cover the hired Cavalier when he first came to Ashfield. But he really needed a more permanent housing for it, to help protect it from the winter cold and autumnal leaf falls, the one curse of living in a country village. He knew he should put it in the adequately sized garage, but Stephen had not yet decided what to do with the Morris Minor Traveller that still resided inside. Stephen loved cars, particularly old ones that were full of character and style, and he had been amazed the old vehicle, one of the original Minor 1000 series introduced in 1956, previously owned by Hilda's husband, Albert who died in 1981, started up at the first turn of the key found in a kitchen drawer, despite having been sat unused for more than fifteen months. Stephen had fallen in love at first sight with the immaculately kept car and could not bear to part with it. He even drove it around the village during the previous summer. He thought he had a solution, but that would depend on getting planning permission to cover the driveway or part of it, and that was something he planned to do this year.

THE MINER'S STRIKE, which had started in March had not begun to bite yet, and Stephen arrived in Ashfield on Friday, 13th April 1984. It was not an unlucky thirteenth for him, and he got picked up from Gatwick Airport by Jessica, who drove them to Ashfield in animated conversation. It was the first real holiday Stephen had taken since joining HMS Alderney ten months prior. A very brief weekend together in Edinburgh in late November to celebrate Jessica's birthday only served to exchange birthday and Christmas presents, Stephen sending yet another jigsaw puzzle to Harri Jasper with seasonal greetings for her parents.

Easter was just over a week away but the church on Sunday was dressed for Palm Sunday and the children carried their crosses as they filed past the Vicar on their way to Sunday School in the Children's Corner. Harri was excited about Stephen's return, especially at the start of her own school holiday, and had spent the whole of Saturday with him and with Jessica. Harri's parents, Sheila and Roy were grateful to have the day to themselves although the Store stayed open all the morning.

Stephen reviewed all of Jessica's alterations and redecorations in the cottage and was delighted with what she had achieved. He was grateful for her parents' help as well but personal thanks would have to wait until the next weekend, Easter, when they were due to visit. He expected to get pressured as usual by Jessica's dad as to when they were going to marry, but the pair of them were quite content in their relationship as things were.

Jessica planned to take holiday with him until after Easter, but circumstances changed when shocking news erupted.

THE COUNTRY OF Libya under the leadership of Muammar Muhammad Abu Minyar al-Gaddafi, known simply as Colonel Gaddafi, had successfully murdered several Libyan exiles living in the United Kingdom and the Libyan People's Bureau in St James's Square was held to account. The bureaux chief, Moussa Koussa, had been expelled in 1980, and his successor and the cultural attaché were recalled to Libya in 1983. A four-man committee of students who had all been involved in revolutionary activities in Libya took over and soon after gave a press conference at which they threatened continued action against Libyan dissidents.

In March 1984, there were bomb attacks in Manchester and London targeting critics of Colonel Gaddafi. The Libyan government in Tripoli denied any involvement but five Libyans were deported by Britain. In April, Libyan dissidents in Britain -- members of the Libyan National Salvation Front (LNSF) -- decided to stage a demonstration outside the People's Bureau. The staff in the bureaux asked Tripoli how they should respond and were given permission to fire if felt necessary on the demonstrators. This information, while being intercepted by GCHQ, the government's communication headquarters, and MI5, was not passed on to the police or the Home Office.

On Tuesday, 17th April 1984, while marshalling the demonstration for the Metropolitan Police, WPC Yvonne Fletcher was fatally shot by staff in the Libyan Bureau. She was twenty-five years old.

THE NEWS CAME on the radio via the one o'clock news and both Stephen and Jessica sat stunned listening to it. Jessica knew she would have to return to the Foreign Office immediately and Stephen asked her to take him with her so he could call in on Sir Geoffrey Cheeseman's office. They both knew they would be gone a few days.

EVENTS SPREAD TO Libya soon after the shooting, where the Revolutionary Guard Corps surrounded the British Embassy in Tripoli, and elsewhere arrested three British nationals working in Tripoli on unspecified charges. The siege of the embassy was lifted the following day, but the embassy continued to be surrounded by ordinary Libyan people who responded to the news from their government that the People's Bureau in London had been attacked by British police. One of the captured British men was released.

The British government requested access to the Libyan People's Bureau but were denied. The Bureau was besieged by British service personnel including the SAS for eleven days, during which time five more bomb incidents in London occurred, all but one of which, at London Heathrow, were defused. The British Police demanded access to the building in a search for weapons and explosives, and to the staff for questioning, but no one person was ever found responsible for the murder of WPC Fletcher. The Libyan staff were eventually repatriated and a considerable amount of weaponry, including submachine guns, pistols, and a great deal of ammunition, was retrieved from the Bureau. On the same day, the British Embassy in Tripoli was closed and most of the diplomats and all their families were flown back to Britain. A small number of British diplomats, not including Her Majesty's Ambassador, Mr Oliver Miles, moved into the Italian Embassy to help provide a limited service to American, French, and Jordanian citizens, as well as the several thousand British residing in Libya, most of whom worked in the oil industry. All had embassies that were closed and then burnt down by xenophobic Libyans.

In the aftermath that followed, five British men were detained by the Revolutionary Guard in Tripoli and were kept as hostage while Colonel Gaddafi's government demanded the restoration of diplomatic relations with Great Britain, and the release of Libyans arrested on terror charges. Although it would take many months to gain the release of these hostages, official relations between the two countries would remain broken for several years.

"Morning," said Sir Geoffrey when Stephen arrived at the office the next morning. "I can't say it's a good one."

"No, Sir Geoffrey. And do I have you to blame for

my transfer from HMS Alderney?" Stephen thought he'd get this one out of the way early on.

"Well, lad," Sir Geoffrey sounded defensive. "You were a bit out of reach doing two-month tours in the North Atlantic."

"I rather thought I had retired from your work," said Stephen. "I haven't been called upon since the Volkov incident."

"And that's because there hasn't been too much to do, at least, nothing that someone else couldn't manage."

"So, Saigon '82 was my last job."

"But that's about to change!" Sir Geoffrey stated. "This Fletcher incident has got us all rattled and we will need to follow it up."

"I guessed you would," said Stephen. "That's why I'm here this morning."

"Good man." Sir Geoffrey opened a map out on his desk and invited Stephen to study it with him.

"I am sending Bob Ford and Ian Brown to Tripoli today while we can, to help defend the British Embassy there. We'll wait to hear the outcome of the ongoing siege in St James's Square, but I want you, Stephen, to be ready to fly out to Malta on my signal where you will join a small seacraft that will land you at Zuwarah, west of Tripoli and just short of the Tunisian border. Your target is going to be Mustafa Ahmed, whom we have identified as the man most likely to be responsible for the killing of WPC Yvonne Fletcher. I'll show you a photograph of him in a moment. Ahmed is known to be in the Libyan People's Bureau, but we are unlikely to be able to detain him as they will all claim diplomatic immunity. He is a fanatic and thought to have been used in the past to target critics of Gaddafi in several European countries. He would not have thought twice about shooting someone in a British uniform just to earn points with his bosses in Libya."

"Weapons?" asked Stephen.

"You'll find those waiting for you in Malta, along with currency, clothing, and a false passport. I don't want the Gaddafi regime to trace you back to the Ministry of Defence here, but I don't want you to get caught either. You'll be posing as an Italian businessman; they still have a reasonable level of free movement in Libya, and I know you speak Italian."

"Grazie, mio Capitano," mimicked Stephen.

"Yes, well," Sir Geoffrey continued. "I expect you will find Mustafa Ahmed in Tripoli, where they'll be bodyguarding him, but Libya won't be able to resist hailing him as a national hero, given the idealist morality of Colonel Gaddafi. I'd like you to stay in London with that girl of yours. Keep the details of your mission to yourself, but Jessica is surprisingly good at being discreet and I'm sure the Foreign Office has a personal stake in this."

Stephen Lodge took lunch with Jessica Thomson at the Foreign Office canteen and told her he would be staying in London at Sir Geoffrey's leisure. Jessica knew what he was saying but also knew better than to ask. From her point of view, it meant that she would still have her boyfriend to herself for a few more days, although she would have to cancel the Easter weekend plans with her parents. Everywhere in London was tense with the ongoing siege so it was not the best of days.

STEPHEN STAYED AT Jessica's flat for the next week, spending most of his days in Sir Geoffrey Cheeseman's office at the Ministry of Defence. He spoke by telephone to Roy and Sheila Jasper and asked them to apologise to Harri for his absence but "something's come up." The whole country had seen the news, so they understood. Roy especially, with the Volkov incident and his daughter's abduction still fresh in his memory, thought about the part that Stephen might have to play in it.

Easter came and went before Sir Geoffrey gave the signal. The Libyans, claiming immunity as expected, would be released in the next few days and he wanted Stephen to be in place when they were. On Tuesday, 24th April 1984, Stephen Lodge left Heathrow on a Britannia Airways flight to Malta, where he landed at Luqa Airport and was greeted by embassy staff, who kitted him out as Sir Geoffrey Cheeseman had instructed. They drove him to Birżebbuġa in the southeast part of the island where he boarded a fast boat to Zuwarah, a small port less than a hundred miles from the capital, Tripoli. The crossing would take all night, but he should hit land before the dawn.

A freight rail line ran from there to Tripoli which he should be able to reach by the afternoon.

Stephen's false Italian passport named him as Stefano Loggia, which wasn't really hiding a lot but was easy to remember. The document included papers giving him clearance to be in Libya as an engineering consultant to Gaddafi's government and named his home address as Montecatini in Tuscany. When he got to the port of Zuwarah, Stephen found it was extremely easy to bribe his way onto a train into Tripoli, having travelled into the country from neighbouring Tunisia. He knew it would not be so easy to come back but he had a plan for that eventuality. He carried a case full of clothing, engineering documents, and miniaturised examples of pump valves, which disguised the weight of a disassembled L96A1 sniper rifle modelled on a .308 Winchester design, concealed inside the base of his case. No one seemed particularly interested in what he was carrying but he expected this to change when he reached the capital.

It was not hard to find the Bab-Al-Azizia barracks in Tripoli. The "Splendid Gate" compound was known to be the home of Colonel Gaddafi and his family and as he liked to keep himself in the spotlight, it was well signposted. Finding a high building to overlook the compound, where Stephen expected to see his target, Mustafa Ahmed, being greeted by Muammar Gaddafi was the more difficult job. Also, the barracks was home to Gaddafi's personal bodyguards so that traffic and personnel were regularly monitored. But Stephen was skilled at avoiding attention and booked himself into a back street hotel close to the barracks, which was originally built by the Italians and briefly occupied by the British Army in the Second World War. King Idris, who had reigned as the United Nations -imposed King of Libya from 1951 until Gaddafi's uprising in 1969, had used the barracks as a base and a palace was erected fronting onto Palms Street. Gaddafi would extend the compound during his time in office but in 1984 it was still relatively small.

It took Stephen two nights to find a suitable building for his purposes. He managed to get set up on the roof of a corporate office building in Palms Street overlooking what remained of King Idris's palace and watched as soldiers marched about the grounds, preparing for some big event. He was surprised by how easy it was to access the building he was in and get up to the roof, where he found an air-conditioning unit in which he could hide his rifle. He had also been supplied with binoculars and a camera with a telescopic lens.

He had not witnessed his target yet but had seen several over-adorned senior officers, including Colonel Gaddafi himself, walking and talking outside of the palace. Keeping himself incognito, Stephen had not heard any news from London, but Sir Geoffrey had told him to expect action by the weekend. He had gathered from the commotion on the streets on Friday, a holy day for the Islamic country, that the British Embassy had been closed and ransacked, a significant event.

It took until Sunday for the event to reveal itself, and Stephen was surprised by what he saw. The day started for him as usual, accessing his observation site, but today was different. Overnight, several gallows had been erected on the high steps of the palace entrance and, while Stephen watched through his binoculars, a military parade was enacted in the palace quadrangle. Stephen set up his camera and focussed as best he could on the activity in front of him. His sniper rifle lay on the roof next to him.

The parade continued as several senior officers and some foreign looking civilian officials appeared from the portico to the palace. They were followed by Colonel Gaddafi himself who was clearly going to address the crowd before him. Stephen observed that a microphone, speakers, and amplifiers had been set up to one side at the top of the palace steps leading up to the gallows. Then a platoon of armed and uniformed soldiers filed out from a side building and threaded their way through the parading ranks. There were ten of them but between their two lines walked four other men, all of them stripped of their top coverings and bare footed. Their trousers hung loose and dirty around their legs. Stephen watched closely through his camera's telescopic lens, taking several photographs as he did so. He had already picked out Mustafa Ahmed but wondered who the other three were.

The small execution party, for that is what Stephen reckoned they were, came to a halt at the bottom of the steps but then formed a funnel enabling each of their four prisoners to climb slowly towards their gallows. As they did so, Colonel Gaddafi addressed the assembled ranks in his articulate and charismatic way, arousing their emotions with his Arabic rhetoric, which Stephen could not hope to understand but could get the gist of by nature of the performance. As he continued to take photographs of Colonel Gaddafi and the clearly condemned men, he saw that Mustafa Ahmed was the only one of the four to stand proud with his head up. He still didn't know who the other men were, but it looked as if Gaddafi himself was going to fulfil Stephen's mission for him by executing them all.

Stephen was glad to have the southern sun at his back while he focussed on the proceedings. Colonel Gaddafi ended his speech with a rallying cry to the soldiers on the parade ground, who cheered and crashed their rifle butts on the concrete surface in salute of their commanding officer. He then walked in front of his prisoners and turned to face them. He walked up to each one in turn and embraced them, kissing each cheek as he did so. It was only then that Stephen recognised each man had his hands tied to their sides. As Gaddafi stood back from his embrace, he saluted each of them as they were lifted into the gallows by four of their guards while a fifth one placed a noose around their neck before they were allowed to drop. The entire process took several minutes, and Mustafa Ahmed was the last to be hung.

It seemed to Stephen that Ahmed and Gaddafi shared a longer embrace before he too was lifted into his death noose. There was no struggle from any of the dead men, and Stephen concluded that the nooses had been set so that their necks were broken, and they would die almost immediately. Gaddafi held his salute for even longer as Mustafa Ahmed died on the gallows that day, then he turned and held up his arms to direct the assembled soldiers to raise an even louder cheer. Stephen was not the only one taking pictures; he could see a couple of civilians running around the parade and up the steps, snapping as they went and shooting video as well.

When it was all over, Stephen knew he would have to get the photographs and himself back to Britain, but the embassy was now closed. He returned to his hotel, gathered his belongings, carefully hiding away his rifle, binoculars, and camera, and used his disguise as an Italian businessman to access the Italian Embassy and claim consular protection. There he found the small crew of British diplomatic staff, so he identified himself to them. The whole embassy knew what had transpired at Gaddafi's palace that morning and kept him waiting while they checked his credentials. The Italians advised he would have to travel to Benghazi to get a flight to Rome, from where he would be able to return to London. Stephen left everything behind except his photographic film, which was sealed in a diplomatic bag and was back in Sir Geoffrey's office by Wednesday, 2nd May.

"MARTYRDOM."

"I'm sorry?" responded Stephen.

"Martyrdom," repeated Sir Geoffrey Cheeseman. "Islamic theology says that if you die for the cause, you are considered a martyr and you will enter Paradise."

They were standing in his office just an hour and a half after Stephen had landed at London Heathrow from Rome and the photographic film he had brought back from Tripoli was already being processed in the laboratories kept in the basement of the building.

"Gaddafi knows when to suck up to the rest of the world and he has already expressed his "regret" for what happened to WPC Yvonne Fletcher to the newspapers and on TV. As a way of currying favour -- which isn't going to work by the way -- he said he would deal with those responsible when they were returned to Libya and he has, but on his own terms.

"We'll get your pictures developed but I expect they will show the four men that were executed are the same four "students" that were appointed to lead the Libyan People's Bureau in St James's

Square. We already know Mustafa Ahmed was one of them, sheltering from the diplomatic storm over his presumed involvement with the March bombings in Manchester.

"He's a clever man, Gaddafi. In Islam, by executing those four men he commits their souls to martyrdom for his cause and that way he wins favour with his followers while to the world he is doing what he promised."

"It doesn't wash with me though, and I can't see that it will impress Margaret Thatcher or her government."

"At least we got our man," said Stephen, "one way or another, and I for one am grateful at the way it happened. It would have been an easy shot but difficult to extricate myself from the melee that followed. And now, I'll go back to Ashfield for the few days Leave I have left. I'm due to report to Portsmouth on the 10th as I'm sure you are already aware."

"Aah yes, but I'm sure we will meet up again soon enough," Sir Geoffrey said, dismissing Stephen from the debrief they had just had. "Mind how you go."

Chapter 4

Ashfield, Dorset

STEPHEN'S OWN CAR was still in Ashfield so he borrowed Jessica's with a promise to return at the weekend when he would pick her up. No, he didn't want to see her parents then; he just wanted the weekend to themselves, thank you.

He only had a week of leave left so he decided to progress his planning application to extend the garage part way down the drive and that would mean going to Dorchester. He knew it would take about eight weeks for the process to complete and he wanted the job completed before the autumn, so he dug out the plans that he had prepared while being at sea on HMS Alderney, and set off on his first day back, Thursday. Jessica had canvassed his neighbours for him, she had more charm than he did, and the nearest ones had signed away any objections having viewed the draft plan that she showed them, although one or two said they would prefer, if anything at all, to see just a roof over a car port.

Stephen used occasions like this to see more of the countryside, so he drove his Viva SL to the village of Ansty and onwards over the Downs to Milborne

St Andrew where he passed the Royal Oak pub and thought it might be a good place to come back to for lunch. He wasn't in a rush, but it only took him forty-five minutes to reach Dorchester where he parked in a car park near the County Hall in Colliton Park. He had telephoned ahead and made an appointment with the planning office managed by Ms Teresa Parker and didn't have to wait long for his appointment.

"You have your draft plan drawn up already, Mr Lodge," Ms Parker said when they had sat down. "Of course, we will have to ask the county surveyor to visit the property and take soundings from your neighbours to see if there are any objections to your plan."

"But I have already canvassed my neighbours and include their written responses in my submission." Stephen couldn't understand why that needed to be done again and was worried that the project would be delayed beyond the summer.

"Even so," said Ms Parker with a calming smile, "it's just part of the process we go through. The county surveyor will come and review the site, and you might be required to submit a proper architect's plan once we've agreed on the scope of the project."

"Well, I hope that can be done soon," said Stephen. "I am a serving RN officer and I report to Portsmouth next Thursday so, what are the chances of getting your surveyor out before then, please?"

"I'll have to confirm, Mr Lodge, but I think we

can do next Tuesday, if that's all right? Of course, this is only the start of the process, and it might be that Mr Turner, our surveyor, needs to return later."

"That could be awkward," Stephen thought aloud, and went on to say that Portsmouth was a new posting for him, and he would not know until he got there which ship if any he was being drafted to. "But I'm grateful for the Tuesday offer, and I am sure we can come to some arrangement about the rest of it. My target is to try and complete the build before the autumn leaves start to fall. I'm new to the countryside, an urbanite by experience, and I've only been in Ashfield for eighteen months. I want to build something in keeping with the local environment."

"I see from your plans that you already have a garage on the property so why not simply store your vehicle in there?" Teresa Parker was curious.

"Aah, well," Stephen explained, "I bought the Farthing Corner House on the passing of Mrs Hilda Smith and, "inherited" you could say, everything in it. That's another story but one thing I absolutely love is the Morris Minor Traveller that belonged to her husband Albert, and that is parked in the garage, where I would like to keep it for protection against the elements, except for the summertime when I plan to drive it around the village."

"I can understand your thinking, Mr Lodge. My dad had one of those when we were kids and used to take us down to the seaside in it."

"He adored that car," she added wistfully, "and

cleaned and polished it every week. Well, I'm sure it's all going to work out eventually, so I'll confirm Tuesday with Mr Turner and give you a call. Tomorrow morning be okay?"

"Tomorrow morning will be fine," replied Stephen, realising the meeting was over. "But not the afternoon. I must drive up to London to collect my girlfriend."

"Tomorrow morning it will be," said Ms Parker, standing ready to shake Stephen's hand and show him out.

STEPHEN RETURNED VIA Milborne St Andrew and took lunch in the Royal Oak. He was apprehensive about the whole planning process but recognised that life in the countryside flowed at its own pace so resigned himself to waiting for the outcome. At least there was a good chance he would see the surveyor before he had to report back to the Navy and he was still confident that he could get the project completed before October, his target month.

As was his liking, he drove on the A354 towards Winterborne Whitechurch, wanting to see as much of Dorset as he could manage in the short periods he had in Ashfield. He knew there were many Winterborne villages, but this would do for a start, and he parked up at the local pub, the Milton Arms, another habit of Stephen's, from where he could go for a walk around the village.

The village was even smaller than Ashfield,

less than seven hundred residents according to a parish poster he found in the entrance to the delightful village church of St Mary's. According to its history, proudly included in a booklet in the church, the non-conformist preacher John Wesley, grandfather of John and Charles Wesley (the founders of Methodism), was appointed Vicar of Winterborne Whitechurch by Oliver Cromwell's Commission of Triers in 1658 but was imprisoned in 1662 for not using the Book of Common Prayer. Preacher John delivered his farewell sermon to a weeping audience. There was a well-used hall in the village, several thatched cottages, and a small Church of England primary school almost identical to Ashfield's. Stephen thought that Ashfield was better but it's a question of what you're used to. Winterborne Whitechurch was kept exceptionally clean, and the gardens were tidy and attractive, and he was reminded that the front garden at Farthing Corner House still needed working on, something he had no experience with.

STEPHEN DROVE BACK to Ashfield across Stillmoor and Tolworth Down and then descended Ashfield Hill on his way into the village. He saw a small flock of Dorset Down sheep on the Fennel Farm owned by Thomas Walker and wouldn't have known what they were a year ago, but he'd been learning. Come to think of it, Mr Walker only had cattle grazing on his land the year before, so these must be new. He popped into Jasper's General Stores for milk, bread, butter, and eggs just before Harri was due home from school. He wasn't the best cook in the world, but he could manage an omelette, which reminded him to get some cheese. He chatted with Sheila, hoping to see Harri when she came home but Sheila warned him that he was not in her daughter's good books, having come home from Scotland in time for her Easter holidays and then disappearing just as quickly. Harri's father, Roy, had tried to explain to her what had happened in London but "kids were kids, and she [Harri] was very disappointed."

"Also, something else has happened," continued Sheila. "She went back to school on Monday only to find out that one of her favourite teachers has died. There's no mystery about it. Reports are that John Cartwright was very overweight and suffered a heart attack probably because of his obesity, but Harri insists that he was killed! You know how fanciful she gets in her imaginings."

"How old was this John Cartwright?" asked Stephen.

"Fifty-one," came Harri's reply as she walked in the shop door, her long brown hair coming loose as she pulled the scrunchy from it. "He was a good teacher, a real laugh, and all the kids loved his funny ways. He was fair-minded too, and patient. Didn't shout when we got something wrong. And I don't believe he just died!" Harri concluded.

"Where did he live," Stephen asked Sheila, "and

was he married?"

"Ashdown apparently," she replied, "but I don't know enough about him to answer all your questions."

"And what makes you say, Harri, that he didn't just die?"

"You'll love this," Sheila said quickly, at which point Harri stared angrily at her mother.

"No one will believe me!" Harri said loudly and emotionally. "Mr Cartwright was fine until we broke up from school before Easter. Yes, he was fat. We all called him Haystack because he had very blond, very untidy hair, but he was all right. He would take us for nature rambles. He took games and P.E. And he always kept a watch out for us at playtimes, joining in the ball games that were played. He was … fine!"

"And so, you think he was killed?" asked Stephen again. "What makes you say that?"

"It's the tramp." replied Harri.

"A tramp?" questioned Stephen.

Sheila interrupted before her daughter could speak. "There's been a tramp, a traveller, seen around the village. That's not so unusual, a bit early in the season but we're used to seeing them passing through the village, looking for casual work on the farms and then moving on towards the coast for the summer trade."

"But this one's been hanging around for weeks," said Harri. "And would always be standing across the road from the school at lunchtimes, watching us kids play. Mr Cartwright spoke to him once or twice and he always left, but he always came back."

"And did Mr Cartwright report this … tramp to the police?"

"I don't know," Harri was getting wound up. "But Police-Sergeant Blake from Ashdown doesn't seem interested in what I've got to say!"

"We called him," explained Sheila. "But Harri's right, and Sergeant Blake wants to wait for the coroner's report before taking any further action. And the inquest won't be held until the week after next."

"By which time," said Stephen, "I will have had to report back for duty. Albeit not so far away this time hopefully. I'm going down to Portsmouth."

"You had better tell Mr Lodge what you've told your father and I about this tramp," Sheila said to her daughter. "Maybe then he will understand why the policeman doesn't go along with your story."

Stephen looked at Harri, while she stared at her mother. "You don't believe me either!" she spat out, crying, and ran out to the stockroom and up the stairs to their flat above the store. They heard the door slam.

"Shall I?" asked Stephen, waving a hand in Harri's direction.

"No, please, leave her," responded Sheila. "She's been like this all week, but she'll calm down. Roy will be home later, and he always manages to lift her spirits. He's changed a lot since Harri's abduction the year before last."

"So, what was it she told you both that you just can't believe?"

Sheila drew herself up. "Harri says the tramp is 'the bad man that kidnapped her.' The Russian, Nikolai Volkov! It's not that we don't believe her, but it's just not possible. Is it."

Stephen was stunned to hear this news, but he had to agree with Sheila and Roy: it just wasn't possible. Nikolai Volkov, as far as he knew, was still being held in prison.

"And he hasn't returned this week. The tramp, that is?"

"So far as I know," said Sheila, "he hasn't been seen in the village since the children broke up for Easter."

STEPHEN TOOK HIS shopping back to the cottage and made sure everything was ready for the weekend. He would be picking Jessica up tomorrow, keeping her car on the driveway so that she could return to town in it on Sunday. He decided he would go up to the Greene Dragon and have a chat with Tim Marshall and find out what he'd heard. Tiny Tim as he was known was ex-Army and they got on fine after a shaky start when Stephen first came to the village. It was a standing joke between them that Tim fancied the pants off Jessica, and Stephen's girlfriend loved to tease him. But there was nothing serious in it. Stephen acknowledged that Tim was incredibly good at organising folk, and if anyone had their ears to the ground it would be the proprietor of the immensely popular and only pub in the village.

"HEY, STEPHEN," SAID Tim. "I heard you were back in town."

"The jungle vine still works then," Stephen responded. "I only got in last night. I'll have a pint of Huntsman, please."

"Good Dorchester ale, that. Is your missus coming down this weekend?"

"Still taken a shine to her then," joked Stephen. "Yes, Jessica will be down tomorrow."

"Aah, well, I'll keep my place in the queue." Tim chuckled. "Always the best man and never the groom."

"Och, you big lug," Stephen had picked up the Scottish colloquialism while stationed at Rosyth. "But I wanted to talk with you about this tramp that's been hanging around. See what you know?"

"Huh, you've been listening to little Harri Jasper. But, yes, there has been one. That's not too unusual once we've got past Easter, but he has kept himself secret. Usually, the travellers are looking for casual work, anything that's not too strenuous and paid in cash so they don't deal with banks or the taxman. I've used them myself when the beer cellar needs a good clear-out or the yard's in a mess, and every year they trim up the edges of the car park for me. But this one hasn't offered his services at all."

Stephen supped his beer. "So, there might be

something in what Harri said: that he's just hanging around watching the school?"

"You're thinking about John Cartwright? I've heard the story, but I can't see anything in it. John popped in here occasionally, although he lived in Ashdown. He'd say he'd had a difficult day with the kids, and he needed a pick-me-up before driving home, where he lived alone, then he'd have a Mendip Twister and a whisky chaser. I hadn't seen him for a while, not since the February half-term, even though he would park every day in my car park. I didn't mind, made no difference to me during the weekdays. But he wasn't in the best of health; carried far too much weight if you asked me."

"Yet the children loved him, according to Harri," Stephen told him.

"And I can believe it. John was a professional, a real teacher by vocation, and he loved his job. He was a local, lived all his life in Ashdown, but he was a big softee. And I mean big, and just a little bit effeminate if you know what I mean. The kind of bloke that the Army likes to toughen up rather than appreciate their talents."

"Do you think he was gay. A homosexual?" queried Stephen.

"Possibly, but I'd only say possibly. But not a threat to those kids, though. He wasn't a child molester, like, but I'd never known him be with a woman although he was friendly with them, and he was fifty-ish without once being married. Devoted to his work I would say, and it's a real shame that he's gone now."

"Thanks for the background. I'll have another Huntsman and then I'll be on my way. I'm sure that Jessica will drag me out for a meal on Saturday or Sunday, so we'll see you then."

Stephen went to sit in a corner while Tim served other customers. He had a lot to think about, especially Harri's assertion that the "tramp" was the Russian, Nikolai Volkov, but he could not see the connection with Mr Cartwright's passing. He could give Sir Geoffrey a call regarding Volkov, and maybe get clearance via him to ask the local pathologists a few questions about the causes of John Cartwright's death. Stephen was inquisitive by nature and cautious about events that occurred coincidentally. A fatalist perhaps; there had to be a reason for why things happen.

THE CALL FROM the Dorchester planning office came through early on Friday morning, when Ms Teresa Parker confirmed the surveying arrangements for the following Tuesday.

"Mr Turner will be with you by ten o'clock so please make sure you are at home and available," Ms Parker instructed.

"Yes, Ma'am," Stephen responded, and then decided he would drive up to London early to see Sir Geoffrey if he could and pick Jessica up on her day off.

When he got into town, he used his permanent

visitor's pass to park in the Foreign Office car park, and then walked down Whitehall to Sir Geoffrey's office.

"Hello, Stephen," Hazel Eaves, Sir Geoffrey's secretary greeted him. "You've not picked a good day. Sir Geoffrey is out at an interview with *his* bosses. I think they are trying to persuade him to retire, but I hope that doesn't happen anytime soon. I've got a few more years to go myself and I don't fancy spending that time training yet another manager to do things the way I like them done." She smiled.

"That's a pity," said Stephen, "that he's out, I mean. I'm sure you'll be here for years to come, Hazel, and I wouldn't like to see the old boy out of the door myself. But I do need to find out something so, could you ask him for me: is Nikolai Volkov still being held in prison? Monday will do for the answer. Sir Geoffrey can call me at the cottage."

"The Russian that abducted that child?" said Hazel. "I can give you the answer for that one. No is the answer. Nikolai Volkov was repatriated to Russia last August, under a deal done through the Foreign Office, I believe. I'm surprised that Jessica hasn't told you about that, she must be involved in that."

"Jessica can be incredibly discreet," but Stephen was surprised. "Especially if it was a deal done secretly. We try not to pry into each other's business too much."

"Why are you asking?" Hazel was curious. "Has

Volkov resurfaced?"

"I don't know," said Stephen, "but Harri Jasper seems to think so. You'd best get Sir Geoffrey to give me a call, if not this evening then Monday first thing, please."

"All right. I'll ask him, but don't expect too much from him today. He's got enough worries with the hounds who want him to retire."

"I'll hope to see you again soon," said Stephen, "even though I've got to report to Victory Barracks in Portsmouth by next Thursday. I have no idea where they're sending me after that."

"Bye for now, Stephen," Hazel said cheerfully. "I'll speak to Sir Geoffrey for you."

STEPHEN LEFT THE office, retrieved his car from the Foreign Office and drove to Chelsea to meet with Jessica. Finding her in good spirits, they took lunch in the Fox and Pheasant just off the Fulham Road, and then Stephen drove them both to Ashfield for an enjoyable weekend to themselves. He did not tell her about Harri's revelations, or fantasy, but she'd soon find out when they went to St Joseph's on Sunday.

REVEREND JAMES ST Johns, the Vicar of St Joseph's, was glad to see them both on Sunday.

"You went missing for a week or two," he said to Stephen. "No sooner were you back (from Scotland) than you were gone again."

"Yes, well, the Libyan thing when Yvonne Fletcher

was killed meant that Jessica had to return to her work at the Foreign Office, so I stayed in London to support her."

"The Foreign Office?" the Vicar seemed surprised. "I didn't realise that Ms Thomson worked there. It's funny how we meet so often yet know so little about what we do in our private lives."

"You're a fine one to talk, as Mrs Smith might say," retorted Stephen. "Hardly anyone knows anything about you, Vicar. And you've lived here a long time."

"Yes, well, I keep up the Lord's work. I don't want to make anything of myself."

"Do you know anything about this John Cartwright business?" asked Stephen.

"Business? What … business? I do know I have been asked to conduct his funeral, when the coroner releases the body, that is. Mr Cartwright's family has asked me to do that because his own vicar refused, which I find curious, but I am not about to question. The funeral will be at the local crematorium, and I am the chaplain there, so I suppose that's why."

"I expect so," said Stephen guardedly, "It's a sad business though, losing someone from the community at any time, and a very popular teacher from what I'm told."

"I don't know much about him," said James St Johns, "but I'll be meeting with his sister during the week. He's only got the one I believe, and an aging mother who lives in a nursing home. They're both in Sturminster Newton."

"Well, I hope it all goes smoothly. The inquest I'm told won't be until the week after next. Will that delay you?"

"Once the coroner releases the body, I can plan the funeral. Understandably, the school have asked to be kept fully involved."

"Of course," said Stephen in conclusion, "And don't expect to see me next week. I'm due back on duty with the Navy this Thursday coming."

Stephen left to gather Jessica, who had been chatting with Sheila Jasper and Jane Kemp, and went to the Greene Dragon for lunch.

Chapter 5

Questions without Answers

"GOOD MORNING, STEPHEN," Sir Geoffrey Cheeseman was on the telephone. It was nine o'clock on Monday morning.

"Hello, Sir Geoffrey," replied Stephen. He and Jessica had had a good weekend together, but she had returned to London the night before.

"I understand from Hazel that you have been asking about Nikolai Volkov," continued Sir Geoffrey. "I'm surprised you did not know already. How very remiss of me but, yes, Volkov was sent back to Russia last August in exchange for two of our agents the Russians had held for a time."

"But why do you ask now?"

"You'll remember little Harri Jasper?" said Stephen. Sir Geoffrey affirmed. "Well, she reckons that a tramp who has been watching her school is Nikolai Volkov, or 'the bad man who kidnapped her' as she puts it. Of course, no one believes her. It's not possible they say, I said it too, but now, knowing he's a free man, anything is a possibility."

"But unlikely," Sir Geoffrey was not convinced. "Why would Volkov return to the scene of his crime, where he might readily be spotted?"

"It seems that here," Stephen replied, "they are so used to tramps or travellers passing through the village, that they don't take a lot of notice of them. Sometimes, they ask for work, casual labour so long as it pays cash, but otherwise they just drift through. This one though seems a bit different: he's been around a while, kept himself to himself, and Harri is convinced it's Volkov."

"But why come back to Ashfield?"

"Because I'm here?" Stephen conjectured. "Because he has unfinished business with me?"

"But you haven't been there. Not until recently that is."

"I know that, but he wouldn't, and that might be why he's hung around."

"He would have to have somewhere to stay?" said Sir Geoffrey. "He could be sleeping rough, I suppose, but that doesn't sound like Volkov's style."

"Aah, well, this is where the rest of the story comes in," began Stephen. "A teacher from the local school died over the Easter holiday, and Harri Jasper thinks that Volkov killed him."

"What!" Sir Geoffrey, aroused. "Whatever gives her that idea?"

"Apparently, John Cartwright, the teacher who died, had to chase off this tramp once or twice when he was seen near the school. That might have made him a target."

"But is there any evidence to support that? How

did this John Cartwright die?"

"No evidence at all. John Cartwright was very overweight and seemingly died of a heart attack. The pathology, I am told, supports that and the police have no interest in his death at all. There will be a coroner's inquest next week but, with nothing suspicious, it will be a straightforward hearing."

"But you are not convinced."

"No." Stephen was ticking off his fingers. "John Cartwright was only fifty-one years old. Despite his size, he was considered a fit man by the school, used for a lot of their activity classes: nature walks, P.E., games, and in the playground that he watched over a lot of the time, he would join in the kid's ball games. I know we only have the judgement of a child, sir, but from what Harri has told me I don't see this guy suddenly dying from a heart attack, and given her recent experiences, she is probably the one person that will look more closely at strangers passing through the village."

"But, if he was that fat, Stephen?" Sir Geoffrey had listened to his reasoning. "A coronary could occur at any time."

"Yes, and the pathology would show the possibility of that occurring, but there is no report of that. I think the local pathologist has just accepted what seems inevitable without looking for anything else."

"I think I see what's coming," said Sir Geoffrey. "But go on, finish your story."

"Tim Marshall at the Greene Dragon tells me

that John Cartwright had changed his habits in the last couple of months, when he stopped going into the pub at regular intervals after school for beer and whisky after a 'tough day with the children.' Where he was well liked by the way; the kids loved him, nicknamed him Haystack and apparently Mr Cartwright never complained. I think also, from something that Harri said, that he might have known this "tramp" and that is why he was able to shoo him away from the school so easily. Tramps and travellers are often times more objectionable, protesting that they are innocent of any suspicion."

"It is possible that John Cartwright might be homosexual. No threat to the children, I am told, but I wonder if he was the one who put up this tramp, and if the tramp was at the school looking out, not for the children, but for Mr Cartwright?" Stephen concluded.

"Has this tramp been seen recently," asked Sir Geoffrey, "And, dare I ask. Do you want to investigate further?"

"He hasn't been seen since the kids broke up from school for Easter. And, yes," said Stephen, who only had three days before he was due to report to RN Portsmouth, "In the brief time I have left of my Leave, I do want to nose around. At the very least, I would like an investigative autopsy done on John Cartwright's body to prove the 'heart attack' was just a natural occurrence."

"I can arrange it," said Sir Geoffrey. "Of course, it

will cost, and the results won't be known probably before you go down to Portsmouth. But what do you want them to look for? You must have something in mind, and I can maybe sell them your idea to help speed up the autopsy."

"I want them to look for an injection mark directly into the heart. Something that would not be spotted except under close examination."

"But the path lab has already ruled out poison, surely? That would have shown up on the first post-mortem."

"No poison," said Stephen, "Bear with me, but something that can't be seen."

"Can't be seen! Whatever are you on about, lad?"

"Air!" Stephen responded, "It's all around us, yet you cannot see it. It's a technique that I've learned about in the field. Inject a person's heart with a small drop of air, causing an air embolism, and nine times out of ten they'll be dead within minutes."

"Not something you've done, I suppose?"

"Me, no. I prefer the long rifle. But I know of it, and it originates with the Russians. It's just a niggling theory in my head, and I'll be happier if it's ruled out, but I would like it looked at."

"And what are you going to do while waiting for the autopsy results, Stephen?" Sir Geoffrey asked, "I know what you're like when you get restless ... as you are."

"I am going to see Mr Cartwright's sister, Joan. She lives in Sturminster Newton, not far from here, and has asked our Vicar, Reverend James St Johns, to conduct John's funeral, which is odd in itself because John lived in Ashdown, but the Vicar there has refused to do it."

"You said this Mr Cartwright might be homosexual. An unwarranted comment from the clergyman perhaps?"

"Perhaps. But I don't know. That's one of the questions I have for sister Joan. I'm going there later this morning with our Vicar."

"Well, we'd best both get on," said Sir Geoffrey, concluding their telephone conversation. "I'll do what I can, re a second autopsy, and get back to you as soon as possible. Keep me posted about your interview with Miss Cartwright, please?"

"I will," said Stephen as he rung off.

STEPHEN HAD ASKED the Vicar when he was at St Joseph's if he might go with him when he next visited Joan Cartwright, and James St Johns told him it would have to be the next day, Monday. Stephen said he could drive them there and the offer was accepted. Joan Cartwright, Stephen was warned, was a forthright woman, who would decide for herself if he, Stephen, was acceptable to attend the interview, but the Vicar thought the fact that Stephen was a serving officer in the Royal Navy would help.

Joan Cartwright was born and raised in Sturminster Newton and still lived in her mother's house in Barnes Close, near to where she worked, running the local Museum almost single handed with a little help from volunteers in the high season. Her mother was no longer at home. Elderly and suffering from dementia, Joan had moved her into a nursing home, still in the village, when she could no longer cope with work and the rigours of a demanding home care situation.

The Sturminster Newton Museum, also the Tourist Information office, where the Vicar had agreed to meet Miss Cartwright, was in the Old Market Cross and occupied the Market Cross House, an attractive Tudoresque, thatched property built from Dorset stone. It was a popular place to visit but this was early in the tourist season and Joan decided she could afford to close for an hour so they would be undisturbed. She was a tall woman, over six feet, and quite sturdy. Dark hair tied in a bun and dressed in a two-piece tweed suit with sensible flat shoes, she greeted them when they arrived and was put at ease about Stephen's presence by the Vicar. Joan was interested in what Stephen did for a living, in part because her own father had been in the Merchant Navy during the war, and had survived it, only to die fifteen years later. His premature death was attributed to Malaria caught in the ports of Africa, and Stephen sympathised with her loss but reassured her that he had only once called into Mombasa, Kenya, and was sure that he would not suffer the same fate.

The Vicar led the conversation, wanting to find

out what he could about her brother John and choosing hymns and readings for the funeral. Joan, the older sibling by five years, told him that her brother's body was due for release by Thursday so they could perhaps plan into the following week, but she had been called already that morning to be told a second autopsy had been requested. The Vicar was surprised and commiserated, while Stephen thought Sir Geoffrey worked quickly as usual and kept quiet about his involvement.

"I would think you can still plan the funeral for next week," Stephen said, "Autopsies don't need to take long and from what I gather, there is no mystery about your brother's death."

"You mean his obesity?" Joan said in response. "Yes, John was very overweight, and I often warned him about a coronary. But he seemed so fit and active, although that doesn't always help. It didn't help him anyway."

"But I have to ask the question," continued Stephen, "why has your brother's own Vicar refused to conduct the funeral?"

Reverend James St Johns was not expecting that comment and looked up sharply, as did Joan Cartwright, who now stared at Stephen with some intensity.

"Why do you ask such a question, Stephen?" said the Vicar, "I am sure my colleague at St Andrew's (the Ashdown church) is just too busy and did not want to hold up proceedings."

Joan though, knew what her answer should be. "My brother was a homosexual, Mr Lodge. The Vicar at Ashdown was constantly preaching at him about his 'wicked ways' as he put it and simply refused to have anything to do with John outside of church."

"That's why my brother moved out of Sturminster. Mum and Dad could not understand John's 'sexual peculiarities,' Dad in particular, and asked him to leave as soon as he was old enough to be responsible for himself."

"My brother was a good man. He loved children but would never impress himself upon them. He was a teacher through and through and safeguarded children, I think, from what happened to him as a child. Early sexual abuse, Mr Lodge, has a way of scarring the soul, and John was determined that he would never inflict that on or allow that to happen to a child in his care."

Reverend St Johns and Stephen listened intently but did not interrupt.

"My brother," Joan Cartwright continued, "lived the rest of his life in Ashdown. He didn't want to be too far away, and when Dad died he was upset that they had never resolved their relationship. He visited Mum after that time at least once a week, and she gradually accepted him for who he was, although never for what he was."

"Did he live alone?" asked Stephen. "In his own house?"

"Yes, until recently," replied Joan. "He had his

own two-up two-down. He would take in seasonal guests occasionally, but not for any length of time, until a couple or three months ago. Around the end of January, he told me that he had a new 'lodger,' not just someone for a week or two but someone who could be there through the whole summer season. I never met the man. It didn't matter to me, and John didn't need the extra income, but he seemed happy for the first time in years. Then, after the February half-term, his habits changed. We didn't see so much of him and when we did, he was always keen to return home. Like a cat on a hot tin roof, he was, a teenager in his first real relationship. I waited for the bubble to burst, but it didn't, and then we got the news of his death. I haven't told Mum yet; I just don't know how she will respond."

"And you accept the cause of death despite his relatively young age: a heart attack?" asked Stephen.

"Of course. I warned him myself, several times, about a coronary. My brother was fat, Mr Lodge. He wasn't just merely obese. The children didn't call him Haystack just because of his hair!"

"Yet you say he was also fit, that he kept himself active."

"Too much activity, Mr Lodge, and especially when you're nearly twenty-five-stone: something is going to give. The stress on the other organs is going to tell over the years. I'd guess this was just his time."

"Were you told what the second autopsy is about?" asked Stephen. "What they expect to find?"

"Just that 'someone' has asked them to confirm that John did not have Type 2 Diabetes. Scientists these days are keen to tie obesity and Diabetes together, but I am sure that John did not have Diabetes. I am as certain as I can be that my brother unfortunately had a heart attack, from which he died."

"Umm. The Diabetes theory is plausible, I suppose, but quick to resolve I hope, for your sake. I know you'll want to get this funeral done."

"And on that note," said the Reverend, James St Johns, quickly, looking at his watch. "We've taken far too much of your time, Miss Cartwright, and we must be on our way. I'm going to provisionally set a date of Thursday the 17th of May for the funeral. It's the day after the intended inquest but I'm sure everything will be settled by then. Your family is quite small and local. Shall we say, eleven a.m.? If that's acceptable, of course?"

"I'll speak to the funeral directors," replied Joan, "and get back to you this afternoon, Reverend. And Mr Lodge?" standing up and offering to shake his hand, "I guess you just have an inquisitive mind?"

"Yes," agreed Stephen, "You could say that."

AND WITH THAT they were done, but the Vicar dragged Stephen across the road to the White Hart public house rather than just get in the car, where he ordered a pint of Tanglefoot for Stephen and a half of Badger's Brown Ale for himself and sat down in a discreet corner.

"So, what was that all about?" Reverend James St Johns was annoyed and didn't mind Stephen knowing it. "Don't you think that poor woman's got enough on her plate without answering personal questions from someone she hardly knows?"

Stephen weighed up his response, while he supped his beer. How much should he tell? Well, if he was going to say anything at all his usual way was, in for a penny!

"It's possible, Vicar," Stephen began, "and I want you to keep this to yourself; not a word to anyone. It's possible that John Cartwright did not die through natural causes."

The Vicar started but Stephen quickly closed him down. "It's possible that Harri Jasper's abductor, the Russian, Nikolai Volkov, *is* the tramp that has been seen in Ashfield, and might also be John Cartwright's mysterious lodger."

"But how could that be?" James St Johns had a look of disbelief on his face. "Your Russian is in a UK prison somewhere, I thought."

"And that's what I thought too, until last Friday when I learned he had been released through an exchange deal last August."

"So, you think he has returned to our village, lodged with Mr Cartwright to gain access to the school, and might have killed John. For what? What has he to gain?"

"I hope that he didn't kill john Cartwright," said Stephen. "But we won't know until the second autopsy is completed and the results are known."

"You ...?"

"Yes, I requested the second autopsy and, by the sound of it, my boss, Sir Geoffrey Cheeseman, has got right on to it and made it happen."

"Either way," continued Stephen, before James St Johns could interrupt him, "Either way, the official cause of death will stay, that John Cartwright died from a heart attack, which will be correct. It is the cause of that heart attack that I am curious about."

"You suspect foul play? And you don't want anyone to know who this tramp might be, and what he may have done to poor Mr Cartwright?"

"I don't want anyone to panic!" said Stephen, a little sharper than he intended. "I don't want anyone to go looking for this guy and risk getting themselves into a jam. If the tramp is who I think he is, we're dealing with a trained KGB agent who has a history of contract killings on his record."

"But..."

Stephen interrupted him again. "That's why you should leave this to me and my colleagues."

A look of realisation overcame the Reverend.

"We are trained to deal with this," added Stephen, "and I will have to find the tramp whether it is the Russian or not and bring him to justice."

"But shouldn't the local police do that?" said James St John.

"It's above their pay grade," stated Stephen. "Special Branch will get involved again," thinking of Hilda's death and Harri's abduction, "and we will hope to do it quickly and quietly."

"While you're away with the Navy? What do we do then, if we see this tramp again, who doesn't seem to have been around for the last few weeks, by the way."

"I know. He seems to have bolted," said Stephen, "but I don't believe he has gone too far. Ultimately, I believe, his target is me. We have history, Volkov and I, and he blames me for the death of a colleague, so he seeks revenge!"

Reverend James St Johns was stunned into silence, but unsure that Stephen was the target. The two men finished their drinks, then got back in the car to return to Ashfield.

Chapter 6

Time and Tide

THE REST OF the Monday was spent quietly by Stephen. He spoke with Sir Geoffrey again and thanked him for his quick action. In return, he was told that the second autopsy had already been conducted and the results would be made known soon.

Stephen spent the evening watching television by himself but couldn't really settle. He was tempted to go up to the pub but held back and instead wrote out a structured list of events that had occurred and some he expected to happen soon. He was very conscious that he was due to report for duty at Portsmouth in just two days and he knew also that Nikolai Volkov, if it was him, had not been seen in the village for almost four weeks. He hoped it would stay that way but, if John Cartwright was killed as he thinks he was, then Volkov must be found and brought to justice, and he doubted that the local police could manage that.

On Tuesday morning, Stephen remembered that the County Surveyor was due to visit and inspect his plans for the garage extension. He had learned that the existing garage was built of cedar wood and, though this would be more expensive than pine, he was more than happy to pay for cedar to be used on the new build as well. It was sustainable and could be locally sourced, so he thought he had a good chance of getting it past the Surveyor's inspection. He thought also that his draft plan was good and did not expect to hire an architect simply to redraw his own plan again. Stephen had always enjoyed technical drawing when he was at school and hoped that this one would pass muster, but, no matter what happens.

A knock on the front door dead on ten o'clock introduced Mr John Turner to him, and Stephen provided the coffee while the County Surveyor for Dorset got set up on the kitchen table. Stephen had already laid out his draft plan there and Mr Turner perused it while waiting for his coffee.

"I've already had a look down the drive, Mr Lodge, and want to look into the existing garage, please. I notice from your plan that you intend for your 'extension' to be freestanding but to butt up to the existing garage, where you'll remove the doors and put new ones on the front."

"Yes, I wanted to build the new garage without disturbing the old one, just in case there were structural problems caused by age. I don't want to risk damaging it."

"And I am told, Mr Lodge ..."

"Please, call me Stephen."

"That's not my way, Mr Lodge. I am told that the existing garage is in use already."

"Yes," responded Stephen, with disappointment and enthusiasm at the same time. "If you've finished your coffee, come out to the old garage and I'll show you what's in there."

"Bring your plans with you, Mr Lodge," the surveyor got up from the table.

They went out to the garage, where Stephen revealed to Mr Turner, Albert's old but perfectly conditioned Morris Minor Traveller.

"She's a beauty, Mr Lodge, and in the original porcelain green as well. I can well understand why you'd want to keep it, but why have two cars? I understand you are in the Royal Navy, so you're not always at home. It seems an unnecessary extravagance to me and would save you a lot of money if you left the garage as it is and just had the one car. Of course, that is my opinion, and I apologise if I express it too loudly."

"No, no," said Stephen. "I appreciate your candour. This one, the Traveller, I have inherited from a good friend, and the white Viva SL you see on the driveway was my father's, so I have a sentimental tie to both vehicles. But, in practical terms, the Viva is the better vehicle to drive longer distances and it looks as if I will be home-based in Portsmouth while at the same time needing to drive up to London occasionally. The Traveller I want to keep for local drives, especially on summer Sunday afternoons."

"Yes, well, that's up to you," said John Turner as he walked around the inside of the old garage, tapping the woodwork here and there and seemingly listening to the sound of it. "You are truly fortunate, Mr Lodge, because this old place is still as sound as when it was built, and it was built well. No leaks, no draughts coming through the walls, and just enough air to keep everything in perfect order. I envy your inheritance and it would be a shame to spoil it."

Stephen wondered what was coming.

"Let's go outside," said the surveyor, "and I'll show you my concerns and my suggestions for a solution."

They walked up to the front end of the driveway, where Mr Turner asked Stephen to look at the skyline of the old garage.

"As you can see, the garage skyline is adequately high but low enough not to stand out against its setting in relation to your cottage and your neighbour's. The garage is wider than the driveway but only really by a doorpost's width. Now, hold your new garage plan in front of you and try to imagine that one standing in front of the old. What do you see?"

Stephen did as he was asked, standing in the middle of the driveway, and holding his plan out flat in front of him. He couldn't see any problem except his garage would peak slightly higher, about a foot above the old one.

"And the roof would be at a steeper angle!" the

surveyor pointed out. "Your garage, freestanding, confined by the driveway, would be almost a foot narrower than the old one by the time you fix doors to it. And when you look at it from this vantage point, looking straight down the driveway, and this is the view that your neighbours will see, you can imagine this narrower structure just blocking out the old garage, rather than blending in with it."

Stephen already had an idea what was coming but had to ask the question anyway.

"What do you suggest then, Mr Turner?"

"Hire an architect," replied the surveyor. "Don't settle for a car port as some of your neighbour's would suggest; I could give you planning permission for one of those easily, but it would never look like it belongs here. Let's go back inside and I'll show you what I think, merely as a suggestion, mind."

They repaired to the kitchen where, once again, Stephen's draft plan was laid out on the table. John Turner got a bright red draughtsman's pencil out of his case and started drawing on Stephen's plan.

"If we draw a line of the existing garage roof across here," he said, wielding his pencil through Stephen's diagram, you'll see how much and how different the skyline is. I know it's an approximate but I'm a fairly good judge of height and width."

Stephen watched.

"You'll see also that with your narrower garage, even if you lowered your roof to the same height as the old one, your centre line, the ridge, is out of line with the one behind it, and it would be the dickens of a job to get them lined up. You've got an eye for detail and perspective, I can see that from your draft here, but I suspect you have drawn this plan while not being at the house and have persuaded yourself that any new structure must be freestanding, thus preserving the integrity of the cottage and the old garage. Are you thinking that you might sell in ten or so years and the new owners might want to tear down the newer parts?"

"Good Lord, no," replied Stephen, who was fascinated by this man's very candid view of his planned extension. "I have no plans to live anywhere else. In fact, even if I stay in the Royal Navy, they'll retire me at the age of fifty-five and I'll be glad of a place I can call my own."

"Good, good," said Mr Turner. "So, here's what I suggest, but let an architect design it. I know you've got a target of getting the whole job done by the autumn and I can well understand why, and I see no problem with me giving you planning permission if your architect does his job well. I can recommend one or two businesses to you, and a good relatively local building company as well."

Stephen had foreseen there would be a bit of back-scratching going on, but he could accept that if it got the job completed.

"Now," returning to the plan, red pencil in hand, Mr Turner drew a few lines. "If you think of the new section as a complete extension of the old, scarfing the timber one into the other and lining up the roofs, you could buttress one side of the new build into the wall of the cottage – that wouldn't be a problem, I've already looked at the stonework. The outer garage wall would be new cedar that you can 'age' artificially to blend in with the old, then move the old doors forward to front the extension, the width of the driveway allows for that, and bob's your uncle, you have an old new double car garage, which would look as if it's been here for years."

Stephen studied the surveyor's sketched lines across his own plan, fascinated by all that Mr Turner had talked about, and then held out his hand.

"You'd better give me the phone numbers for those architects and builders, Mr Turner, and thank you for your professionalism and your insights. Yours is a much better idea than mine."

The two men concluded their business as friends and Mr Turner assured Stephen he would address the architect's new plan as soon as it arrived in his office.

Time for lunch, thought Stephen after Mr Turner had left, but I'll give Jessica a call first and let her know how everything is going.

JESSICA REMINDED STEPHEN he would have to get his uniforms drycleaned before going down to Portsmouth on Thursday, so a trip to Blandford Forum was in order. He knew it wouldn't take long to drive there and took a detour first to say hello to Plain Jane at her tearoom. Driving to the North

Dorset Railway station, he greeted Jane with a hug. She was still beautiful and a rival to Jessica, but he knew his place and did not play up while he was there. He asked after Eric, her husband, who worked on the North Sea oilrigs off Scotland and was told he would be home in a couple of weeks. He asked after Jane and Eric's older son, Eddie, who was in his last year at Blandford Forum Secondary and was still hoping for an engineering apprenticeship to follow school.

"He'd do well in the Navy," Stephen told her.

"But that would take him away from here," smiled Jane giving him the cup of coffee he had ordered. "And he's still not keen to leave his old mother to shoulder the responsibilities of home life alone."

They both laughed; they'd been down this particular street many times.

"He loves his scooter, though. The one your boss bought for him. He gets to leave later in the mornings and he's home quicker as well. And he gets kudos from his friends at school who envy his trips on the bike. One or two girls as well!"

"Let's hope he keeps up his good schoolwork," said Stephen. "Girls can be such a distraction."

They laughed again.

"As, I am sure, you would know!" Jane grinned at him.

"How are the twins?" Stephen asked. "Have they brought home any stories about Mr Cartwright?"

"The dead teacher? No. Are you expecting

anything?"

"Harri Jasper seems to have taken the news quite badly," said Stephen.

"Yes, well," Jane retorted, "Harri does have a wild imagination. I'm not criticising Sheila or Roy but Harri is left rather too often to make up her own mind on things."

"I guess that's true," said Stephen. "A little understanding and explanation at times like this would be useful. Anyway, I must be off to Blandford. Got to get my uniforms cleaned; I report to Portsmouth main barracks on Thursday."

"You're no sooner here than you're gone again, and we miss you, Stephen." And Jane leaned forward, quickly pecking his nose. "But Jessica's a good substitute, and when she comes up on a Saturday, at least she will help me out with the village kids," referring to the playgroup that met in the tearoom on Saturday mornings while local mothers went shopping. Stephen was surprised by that snippet of news; Jessica had never shown any interest in children while back in London.

HE LEFT JANE to it and drove the six miles into Blandford where he parked up and found a Drycleaner's easily enough. He had to pay extra to guarantee his uniforms would be ready for collection the next day. He could have returned to Ashfield but instead drove down the B3082 to Wimborne Minster. Stephen liked driving and it took less than half an hour to cover the ten miles. He was in time to watch a glass blowing exhibition in one of the small factories and visit the flat-roofed tower of the Saxon-built Minster, which looked more Norman and Gothic, before it closed at four p.m. Set between the Stour and the Allen rivers, Wimborne is an attractive town on a sunny day, with enough shops to keep the customer dry and interested if the weather is inclement.

Stephen visited one or two of the smaller shops by the river and had a good walk about before climbing back into the car and driving to Kingston Lacy on his way home. The estate, owned by the Bankes family of Corfe until 1981, had a very pretty garden and Stephen went there to try and get some tips on what to do with his own front garden. He and Jessica would have to talk it through when they were together at Farthing Corner.

AFTER HE GOT home he put a late call through to one of the architect businesses that Mr Turner recommended and was pleased to get a commitment to a visit the next day. He also called the Vicar and asked if they could meet at the church to talk some more about John Cartwright. Reverend James St Johns was reluctant but agreed to meet at five p.m. on Wednesday for an hour at the Vicarage before the monthly bible study meeting at seven. Stephen thanked him for the opportunity. He took a walk to Jasper's and found Sheila and Harri in the store and stayed and had a chat with them before continuing up through the village to the pub. He knew the weekday pub menu was limited but he preferred it to cooking a meal himself and eating alone.

THE NEXT DAY, Wednesday, the last day of his so-called Leave that seems to have passed too quickly, was going to be busy. Stephen would have to go into Blandford to collect his uniforms, and he was due to meet the Vicar at five in the afternoon, but first he expected a rep from the architect's office to visit.

Ten o'clock came about before the architect arrived but Stephen was not too concerned. Miss Susan Sandhurst, junior partner at Able Architects looked young, but she soon proved worthy of the task when they went outside to review the site for the garage extension and looked at the sketches that the County Surveyor had scribbled on Stephen's original draft plan. With his assistance, Miss Sandhurst took measurements of the existing garage, including the height and position of the ridge relative to the cottage wall, while standing on a ladder she had brought with her, and measured out the length of the extension needed to accommodate Stephen's Viva SL.

"Cedar is a good choice of wood to use, Mr Lodge, but pine is cheaper and could be stained to match the colour of the existing garage."

"But pine would not have the same texture or grain of the cedar and I know it can be stained but it would always look different. Cost is not your concern, Miss Sandhurst, so we'll stick to the use of cedar, please. Time however is, and I want to get the whole project completed before October."

"Okay," said Miss Sandhurst, "If I may, I'll take your draft with Mr Turner's ideas on it and get back to you by the middle of next week."

"Thank you," said Stephen, "but I report for duty with the RN in Portsmouth tomorrow, so I'll give you my girlfriend's telephone number as I don't know yet where I will be. Her name is Jessica Thomson, and she lives in London during the week, and here at the weekend. Jessica can deal with this and keep me posted with the detail."

"Very well then," Susan Sandhurst took the number offered and shook Stephen's hand. "I'm sure that we can progress this quickly, and my office can recommend a local builder who is just right for this kind of job."

Stephen smiled as they parted company. He was certain the architect's office would suggest the same builder as Mr Turner and he jokingly dubbed the three participants as the "Anonymous Backscratchers Club."

HE SAT FOR a while contemplating how things were working out and reviewing the changes he and Jessica had made and were about to make to Farthing Corner House. He loved living here and was glad the cottage retained the feel of Mrs Smith's presence. He knew they still had work to do but Stephen Lodge felt that he and Jessica Thomson could one day settle here, even raise a family, if the Royal Navy and the Foreign Office could ever give them enough time together.

BEFORE HE MET with the Vicar, Stephen had to go to Blandford Forum to collect his clean uniforms. He also needed to shine up his regulation black leather shoes and pack his case. Not for him, a canvas kitbag such as he had when he first joined the Royal Navy as a boy at HMS Ganges in Shotley, near Ipswich. Instead, he had a standard-issue green Pusser's suitcase, the likes of which never seemed to wear out no matter how old it got, and just big enough if packed properly to keep his kit stowed and tidy.

He turned back the rug in the back bedroom, his original bedroom when he boarded with Mrs Smith, and lifted the floorboards to find the Walther PPK that he had bought at Conyers when he first came to Ashfield. The gun was in good order, but he stripped it down and cleaned it anyway. Jessica did not know that he kept a gun in the cottage, and it was best that way. As far as Stephen knew, Jessica had no experience with firearms and a gun in the wrong hands was certainly a dangerous weapon, for the user as well as the target. The Walther was put away where he kept it, the rug was laid over, and Jessica would continue to be none the wiser.

ON HIS RETURN from Blandford, he went straight to the Vicarage where Reverend James St Johns was setting up his generously sized living room ready for that night's bible study group. The Vicar and Stephen went to the kitchen for coffee.

"Do you get many takers?" asked Stephen. "At the bible study, I mean."

"Not enough, really, and mostly women, of course. One or two of the older men accompany their wives, but it is mostly women. They will take over the Church one day." The Vicar looked up optimistically, "You're welcome to stay, Stephen."

"Me? No," Stephen replied, "I've got too much to do before I go back to the Royal Navy tomorrow. An early start as well; I report for duty at 0800 in Portsmouth."

"We don't finish late, but I can appreciate your busy schedule. Time is something none of us ever have enough of and, of course, your leave has been preoccupied with so much to do."

"My Leave has certainly not been the rest-and-recreation period the Navy promised me, but I can hardly blame them. The Libyan siege thing was a nuisance to Jessica, and then we've had this tramp and Mr Cartwright."

"Speaking of that," said the Vicar, "have you had the results of the second autopsy yet?'

"No," replied Stephen. "And I must admit I had almost forgotten about it. It will have to wait for now; I will have to contact my London boss, Sir Geoffrey

Cheeseman once I've settled into wherever the Navy sends me next."

"So, we can probably accept that John Cartwright died of natural causes?" The Vicar said pointedly.

"Yes, I suppose so, or else the path lab would have come back sooner, I guess."

"Good, good," said James St Johns, "because I intend to go ahead with John's funeral next Thursday, no matter what happens. Miss Cartwright has confirmed with the Funeral Directors the date and time, and John's family, as small as they are, are geared up and ready to go. His mother will be attended by two carers on release from her nursing home. I understand she has now been told of her son's passing but I'm not sure how much she understands. Her dementia is quite bad, I believe."

"I wish you well with that one, Reverend. Funerals are not my cup of tea although I've been to a few in the Navy. I'm afraid that losing both my parents at the same time rather blew me and God apart for a time..."

"But you're good now?" asked the Reverend.

"Yes, I'm good now," Stephen was thoughtful. "Thanks to this place mostly: Ashfield, and the people in it. I have found a level of peace. It's so easy here to stroll onto the Downs on a sunny day and forget your worries with the world in the silence of the countryside."

"I understand what you mean," said the Vicar. "I found it so myself when I first came to the village.

What I've never told anyone is that I passed through here before the war, when my parents first sent me to Britain. I always remembered the tranquillity of it and worked hard to get back here as soon as I could."

"What happened after the war?" asked Stephen, thankful for the slight opening he could see through a door that had probably stayed close for years. "Did you go back to Czechoslovakia to find your parents?"

"Yes, but they had disappeared. It took me many years to find out what had happened to them but by then all I could do was mourn their deaths in wartime."

"Were you already involved in the Church, James? You don't mind if I call you James? All this Vicar and Reverend stuff gets me down when I'm trying to have a friendly conversation."

"James will be okay," said the Vicar, "although my birth name is Jakub. Jakub Havel, but I'll thank you to keep that to yourself. James St Johns was the name I was given by my mentor when I entered the Lord's work with the Church of England."

"A bit like being renamed," observed Stephen, "when you become a priest in the Roman Catholic Church."

"You're very astute, Stephen Lodge. When did you first notice my Catholic upbringing?"

"The fact that you come from a catholic country kind of gave you away. Also, the way you conduct your services ... almost High Church ... in a country parish, it doesn't quite ring true."

"That's where you're wrong, Stephen. The good folk of the countryside are very conservative in their thoughts, and also very routine in the structure of their days. Having a church service that they can guarantee will start and finish on time is an especially important part of that routine. Being a vicar of a country church has been the ideal hideaway for a defrocked catholic priest."

"Defrocked?" Stephen was surprised at how wide the Vicar's door had opened. "Where, and why would that have happened?"

"The Russians took over my country, post-war," James began. "They imposed their restrictive practices not just on the people in the street, Stephen, but also on the church clergy. My church of St Vitus in Prague, the biggest and most beautiful church in the country, where kings and queens have been crowned and where our most venerated saints are buried, was subsumed by the Russian Orthodox Church who have always supported their leaders, and I could not allow for that to happen. So, I became first a protestor, and then an outcast!"

"And you left your country and came back to England. But why join the Church of England? Why not your own brand of Christianity, the Catholic Church?"

"Because I had to hide, Mr Lodge! Because when the 1956 uprising was crushed by the Russians in our neighbouring country, Hungary, I joined the action on the streets of my own country and fought back against their brutal oppression. Because by doing so," James St Johns was almost in tears, "I might have killed for my country, but not for my God, and I don't know that he will ever forgive me."

"And you've kept quiet about this ever since," Stephen wasn't sure what to say.

"Of course! Do you broadcast what you do, Stephen, other than being in the Royal Navy? You don't tell everyone that you are in fact a contract killer, an assassin for Her Majesty's government. And yes, before you wonder, I have spoken with Roy Jasper, who needed a lot of prayer and counselling after his daughter's abduction and his part in her rescue."

Stephen was stunned.

"I have hidden myself away in Ashfield," continued the Vicar, "because the Czech *Státní bezpečnost*, the StB or secret police, are still after me for the 'crimes' as they see it, that I committed when I stood against them with many of my countrymen in opposition to the Russian occupation of our motherland. Should I ever die unexpectedly, Stephen, it will be because of the Czechoslovakian STASI. Just look to my diaries for clues."

"The Communists have systematically, over countless years, oppressed the Czech and Slovak people of my homeland. Look what happened in 1968, when Alexander Dubček introduced liberal reforms to democratize our politics, our country! Even in front of the world's cameras, a Warsaw

Pact army invaded Czechoslovakia and swept those policies aside as if they were nothing. Did the United Nations stand up to the Union of Soviet Socialist Republics? No! They made a whimper of a sound but could not risk a war with Russia."

"Look what happened to Jan Palach and Jan Zajic who burned themselves to death in Wenceslas Square in protest against those armies invading their country. When you belong to the Soviet Union, Mr Lodge, there is only one rule, obey Russia! There is only one ruler, the so-called President of the USSR. You do as you are told, or you die! And I am afraid of death, and I have hidden myself away in Ashfield all these years, but I have stayed connected with my fellow protestors who continue the fight."

"So, when you mentioned the other day about the KGB agent, Nikolai Volkov, possibly returning to Ashfield, I thought it might be me he is after, not you."

Stephen sat quiet for several minutes. He considered everything the Vicar had told him, and couldn't help but feel sympathy for the poor, wretched, man sat in front of him. He had come seeking knowledge of the Reverend James St Johns but was astonished at all that Jakub Havel had said. It was as if the man in front of him had uncorked a bottle and poured out its entire contents. The only thing that Stephen could do was take James's hands into his own and pray for the Vicar's survival.

"You asked me on Monday what you should do if

the tramp, whoever he might be, reappeared in the village?" said Stephen. "I will give you Sir Geoffrey Cheeseman's personal number so that you can ring him instantly. You will not put yourself in peril. Sir Geoffrey has an arrangement with the Royal Navy that I shall be freed from my duties wherever I am, and I will come home quickly and do whatever is necessary to keep you and everyone else safe."

"Now, I want you to sort yourself out, calm your emotions, and go about your business as if we'd never had this conversation. And, trust me, I will never speak a word of this to anyone."

STEPHEN DROVE TO his cottage deep in thought at what the Vicar had said to him. He remembered the Reverend's own words just the past Sunday, "It's funny how we meet so often yet know so little about what we do in our private lives." He now knew so much more than he could have expected about James St Johns, and the Vicar in turn knew about him. It was in their mutual interest to say nothing about each other, but Stephen knew what human nature was and the truth would out one day. He could only hope that it would take many years and that he, Stephen, would have left the Royal Navy and the Ministry of Defence well behind him by then.

As he parked his car in the driveway he could hear the telephone ringing in the house, and he hurried indoors to answer it, hoping it would be Jessica. But it wasn't and he was disappointed.

"Hello, Sir Geoffrey," Stephen had a caller ID on his hall telephone, another modern introduction to the house. "Have you called just to wish me well for the morning."

"I am sure the Navy will find you plenty to do when you get to Portsmouth tomorrow, Stephen." Sir Geoffrey responded. "No, I have called to give you the results of John Cartwright's second autopsy."

Stephen's senses went up. "Already! Please tell?"

"Unfortunately," began Sir Geoffrey, "you were right. John Cartwright died of cardiac arrest due to an air embolism, which was caused by party or parties unknown injecting air directly into his heart." Sir Geoffrey was clearly reading direct from the report he had received only one hour before.

"So, John Cartwright was murdered?" Stephen was not surprised by the news, but he wished it had been otherwise. "Do we involve the police now, or what?"

"No, I think we should keep this one to ourselves. It might come up at the Inquest next week, although I have asked the pathologist to keep quiet about her findings. I have no real authority on that one, but the official verdict for John Cartwright's death will be that he suffered a heart attack due to his gross weight. That could happen to anyone, especially a man of twenty-five stone and questionable domestic habits."

"What I will do though," Sir Geoffrey continued. "I will send a couple of Special Branch officers down to the Royal Corps of Signals camp near Blandford Forum and set them the task of scouring the nearby countryside to see if they can trace this tramp that you've all been talking about."

"Will it be SB1 and SB2 again, sir?"

"As always, Stephen," Sir Geoffrey couldn't help but smile at the generic nicknames. "As always."

"Keep me posted, Sir Geoffrey, if they turn anything up," Stephen sounded weary. "I'll be on tap to return if I am needed here "

"Well, we're going to have to find this tramp." Sir Geoffrey said in conclusion. "A murder has been committed. We don't know who by exactly, but we can have a fairly good guess, and that means we, you, must be on high alert."

And also the Vicar, thought Stephen, just in case he was right and Nikolai Volkov is in fact after him and not Stephen.

Stephen and Sir Geoffrey exchanged pleasantries, and promised to keep in close contact, and then rang off. Stephen wanted to take a shower, knock up yet another cheese omelette and telephone Jessica. He would have to be on the road early to be sure of getting to Portsmouth by eight in the morning.

Chapter 7

Reporting for Duty

VICTORY BARRACKS IN Queen Street, Portsmouth, will always be known as such to the thousands of Royal Naval personnel that have passed through its gates. It wasn't fully used by the Royal Navy, however, until after the Second World War.

Built by convict labour and completed by 1886, the barracks, under the name of Victoria after the reigning monarch, became the home for the 1st Battalion of the South Lancashire Regiment and remained an Army and Royal Marines establishment throughout the First World War, becoming an all-Forces barracks between the two wars.

Stephen Lodge knew it well. He had first come here when he was drafted to HMS Londonderry (F108) as a seventeen-year-old junior rating, when she was in dry dock for refit in 1964 and the crew, lower deck and NCO's were all accommodated in Jervis Block on the east side of the vast parade ground. In those days, the crew mustered on the parade ground every day including weekends and marched down Queen Street into the Dockyard to work on the ship, preparing it for seaworthy trials.

But by now, the barracks had changed. In fact, there was practically nothing left of the original buildings, just the Rodney Block on the western side of the parade ground where in 1967 a new WREN's Quarters had been built. The main gate of the now-renamed HMS Nelson still stood as did the Guardhouse, and it was to this that Lieutenant Stephen Lodge RN reported at 0800 on the 10th of May 1984.

"Please, Sir, come with me," the Leading Hand of the guard said to Stephen, and marched him across the yard to Rodney Block, where the Administration offices were situated. It was a fine day, an early summer's day, and Stephen felt warm inside his No.2 uniform. He had driven from the cottage, setting off at five a.m. to pass through Blandford Forum, Wimborne Minster, Ringwood, and the A31 New Forest road, but had still arrived early. He expected to park in the Officer's Wardroom opposite the main gate of the barracks but was surprised to see it closed, scheduled to be handed over to the University of Portsmouth as an accommodation block. Stephen had to park in a side road, Lion Terrace, until he could find where he was going next.

The main naval base in Portsmouth was commanded by Commodore D.C. Lewis, but its administrator was Captain Brian Moss, who introduced himself to Stephen when he walked into Rodney Block.

"Welcome to HMS Nelson, Lieutenant Lodge,"

the captain returned the salute offered by Stephen. "I understand you've just spent ten months on fishery protection duties off the Faroe Islands. It must have made for a cold winter?"

"In truth, sir," replied Stephen, "It wasn't too bad weather-wise. A couple of storms but mostly bright and sunny. The worst of it was being cooped up on a small vessel for two months at a time with only thirty-five crew and not enough to do. Although the skipper was incredibly good at keeping morale up."

"Duncan Robson. Yes. I know Duncan, we served together as sub-lieutenants on HMS Hermes back in the seventies. A good man, and he speaks well of you, Mr Lodge, according to the report he sent us," Captain Moss waved the file in his hand. "I fear you're going to be wasted here but we have been asked by the MoD to keep you ashore for a few months, so I'm going to base you at HMS Vernon on St George's Road down near the harbour. Do you know it?"

"I've been there, sir," began Stephen, "although I've never been in their barracks when I've passed through Portsmouth before. But what will I be doing there; I had expected another coastal patrol posting myself."

"Orders are orders, Mr Lodge, and ours come from the First Sea Lord. Perhaps they have some grand plan for your advancement. I hear you are in line for promotion?"

"Promotion? Me? I knew I might qualify on a time-basis sooner or later," Stephen had been a lieutenant for more than seven years, "but I hadn't really thought about it, and no one has suggested it to me."

"Well, we shall see," Captain Moss responded. "You are to report to Captain Jonathan Husband at HMS Vernon as soon as you can, and he will outline your work there. Think of it with positivity, Lieutenant Lodge. With the exception of duty watches, you've become a Monday to Friday, nine to five, sailor, and I can tell you, if you have family like I do with the children at school, there are a lot of advantages to it."

"No children yet, sir. I'm not even married, but I'll be glad to get home at the weekends. I have a cottage in Dorset, only bought it eighteen months ago and I haven't been there for a while due to the North Atlantic posting. It will be nice if I can spend some time doing the place up."

"Good luck with that, Lieutenant. I know how difficult it is to establish your own shore base when you're permanently at sea. I'm incredibly grateful to my wife who seems more than capable of skippering her own ship and managing the crew at home. Four kids is enough to handle for any woman alone but that's the price we've paid for my overseas commissions. Personally, I am more than glad for a spot of shore time."

The two men saluted, shook hands, and parted company. Stephen was escorted back to the Guardhouse and out of the main gate to be left to find his car and drive the few streets to HMS Vernon.

HMS VERNON WAS established as a Naval shore base in 1876, although it took its name from the floating ship of the same name that functioned as a school for the early development of torpedo warfare. The ship had been docked alongside the harbour wall for several years and the "stone frigate," as naval shore bases get referred to, grew in size as more classrooms and workshops were required. The barracks, now spread along St George's Road from the Hard to Portsea and hidden behind an unnecessarily high wall, was the first purely Naval base created in Portsmouth outside of the Dockyard itself.

Stephen drove through the impressive main gate of the Torpedo and Anti-Submarine (TAS) school and was directed to where he could park his car and where the Captain's office was to which he should report. No escort this time; he was expected and already cleared by the crew at HMS Nelson, so he walked himself into the office to meet the commanding officer, Captain Jonathan Husband.

Years before, when Stephen first came to Portsmouth having completed his schooling at HMS Ganges, he was based at HMS Dryad in Southwick nine miles outside of the town. Stephen joined the Royal Navy as a signalman but was never fast enough as a typist or when transmitting morse code to pass muster. He transferred to the Seaman Branch and specialised in Radar Plotting, which he excelled at. Several of his friends from Ganges came to Vernon as TAS trainees, and several more went to the Gunnery

School at HMS Excellent on Whale Island. These were all sub-branches of seamanship in the Royal Navy, but while TAS and Radar worked closely together in the Operations Rooms onboard ship, Gunnery went off and did whatever they did. So, it wasn't a complete mystery to Stephen why he should find himself posted here.

"I'm going to put you into our Operations Room, Stephen," Captain Husband told him, "where you can teach our trainees how to interact with other branches. Radar, Signals, Anti-Submarine, even Gunnery these days with precision-target missiles, it's all done there and it's all much the same job."

"Thank you, sir," said Stephen. "I take it I will be billeted on base?"

"Yes, you'll find the Wardroom just along the corridor in what was the Harbourmaster's House, and cabins are available upstairs. We don't have too many officers staying on base. I understand you live in Dorset somewhere, so it won't be practical for you to commute. Most of the officers we have here go home to their wives and families overnight, except the Duty Officer: his cabin is Number One. But you have a look upstairs and I'm sure you'll find something to suit. Just let my secretary know the cabin number."

"Thank you again, sir. I'll bring my case in from the car."

"Oh, and I know this is a bit rich, but I like to throw people in the deep end, so you'll be duty officer this weekend. Okay?"

Stephen smiled. He knew by now the way the Navy worked. "I had expected as much, sir," he said, "that's why I gave the girlfriend the weekend off." Both men chuckled.

"But," said Captain Husband, "and this is a big BUT! You'll be teaching in our school here only for three days a week. Then, Wednesday and Thursday each week for the next three months, you'll be at school yourself as a student at the Maritime Warfare School, and I think you know where that is."

"HMS Dryad, sir. That will be interesting," Stephen was surprised. "What's that about, and where is the Navy planning to send me next?"

"The only thing I do know, Mr Lodge, is that, if you pass your Warfare Officer training, you will be promoted to Lieutenant Commander. Then you might get that sea-posting you'd expected. Congratulations." And Captain Husband gave Stephen a salute instead of a handshake.

STEPHEN WENT BACK to his car to retrieve his case and his No.1 uniform that was hanging from the door-grip inside the rear door, and returned to the Harbourmaster's House cum Wardroom, to find himself a cabin. He chose one at the front because, although it would be noisier with foot and car traffic passing through the main gate, he could keep an eye on his car in the car park and at the same time watch the Wightlink car/passenger ferries going to and from the Isle of Wight.

Warfare training at HMS Dryad for him; teaching kids in Ops procedures here at HMS Vernon: it was going to be a busy three months, and he wondered how long it would be until Sir Geoffrey Cheeseman got in touch. He was the one, Stephen knew, that he had to thank for all of this. He was the one that wanted to keep Stephen on tap for his own purposes. And Warfare training on the cheap to sharpen up one of his "Stags" with no cost to the Cheeseman department, was right up Sir Geoffrey's alley. Stephen smiled as he thought how sneaky his London boss had been, but how clever as well, and if Stephen were going to get a promotion out of it, that would be fine, sir, thank you very much. He resolved to work hard at his training, both as a teacher and as a student.

AND WORK HARD he did. Stephen quickly settled into the HMS Vernon routine, and he found the training of junior seaman in Operations Room procedures surprisingly entertaining. His first trip back to Dryad in almost twenty years was good and he had to accept his Warfare training was going to be beneficial. Nothing else was happening! He had a couple of runs ashore, once to go up to London for the evening by train from the Harbour Station to see Jessica, and he got home to Ashfield once every third weekend. Able Architects had drafted a plan for his garage extension, which he and Jessica reviewed one weekend and then submitted to the Planning

Office in Dorchester for permission to go ahead from the County Surveyor. And Mr John Turner was as good as his word, responding affirmatively and reminding Stephen about the builder he had recommended. Jessica took care of the building project, and the builder, who could start in mid-July, promised to have the seven-week job completed by early September.

There was no news from Sir Geoffrey, although they had talked by telephone. The Special Branch crew based in Blandford had seen and heard nothing. John Cartwright's inquest recorded a natural death by cardiac arrest and the funeral had gone smoothly. No fresh evidence of third parties and foul play had become known. The end of June came quickly, and Stephen began to think the tramp and the teacher incident was something of nothing.

UNTIL ...

Chapter 8

Lingering shadows

ON SUNDAY, THE 1st of July, Jessica travelled down to Portsmouth to spend time with Stephen. There was an ulterior motive to the visit: with Stephen's thirty-seventh birthday coming up in two weeks' time, she wanted to guarantee he would be back in Ashfield where she was arranging a party with his neighbours and friends. It was a lovely summer's day, and they went for a walk on Southsea Common, avoiding the funfair but intending to walk to the Pyramid Swimming pool for a dip. If there was time, they would pop into the D-Day museum as well.

Two lovers on a sunny day, even when they've been in a relationship for a number of years, can be so wrapped in each other's company that they forget to look up from time to time. As it was with these two. They walked across the Common taking no notice of the smartly dressed man in his fifties, wearing a green tweed coat, flat cap, and brogues, using a walking cane to keep him steady on the grass, who dogged their every move.

NIKOLAI VOLKOV HAD been tracking Stephen

Lodge for the last two months. He had altered his appearance as best he could and returned to Ashfield in January only to find that Lodge had not been seen since the previous July. Frustrated by his absence, he had decided to wait as cheaply as possible for him to reappear as he was sure he would, and he'd got lucky when he was able to attract the gay teacher, John Cartwright, into a relationship. It was extortion really: Volkov had persuaded John that he could convince his head teacher and the local education board that he, *John*, had been ogling the small boys in the showers after games and that he might have "inappropriately touched one or two of them." John was sure that being a homosexual man was not a crime, but knew that Simon Anchorman, the headmaster of Ashfield Primary, would take great delight in any opportunity to sack him, and that would prevent him working with children anywhere else. John knew himself to be innocent and teaching was his life, and he could not afford to lose his career or his reputation. So, he'd accepted the situation with his new "lodger," and he had to admit there were some benefits in having another similarly aged man to live with, even if he were not British.

Nikolai Volkov was a Russian. He came from a country where homosexual practices were very much a crime, but that had not prevented him having a long relationship with Pyotr Petrovich, who was not only a colleague in the KGB but was also his lover. Volkov was bisexual but had never settled into a relationship with a woman. With Pyotr it was different because, being men, they could stand the rigours of their very enjoyable sex life and he, Nikolai, had grown to love this man. He partnered Pyotr on many missions abroad and they enjoyed a greater freedom when they did so to demonstrate their love for each other. When Stephen Lodge killed Pyotr in Saigon, he not only damaged Volkov's reputation with his KGB bosses but he took away the love of his life, and now Nikolai sought revenge. He had tried, and failed, to target Stephen himself, when his colleague Dmitri Mikhailov had got himself shot. He felt no pity for Mikhailov: the young and inexperienced agent had put them both in unnecessary danger by killing the old lady, Mrs Smith, and abducting the child, Harri Jasper. But it did mean another loss of face with his KGB employers and Nikolai had been fortunate to be released from an English jail last August after only ten months of incarceration. The terms of the deal were of no consequence to him, but when he returned to Russia and the KGB, he found himself sat behind a desk at headquarters in St Petersburg with nothing to do and not being trusted to take part in active missions.

No one in the KGB headquarters seemed to care if he were around anyway, so he "excused" himself, and returned to the UK to finish the mission that he'd started, to rid himself of the shadow of Stephen Lodge. But he had switched his sights to a new target: Lodge had taken away the love of Nikolai's life, and Volkov would now do the same to him. The death of John Cartwright had been unfortunate but necessary when John himself became too possessive. Nikolai had told John he would be leaving at Easter, and when the Englishman collapsed into a tearful rendition of "everyone I've ever loved turns their back on me," Nikolai coldly decided to put him out of his misery. Of course, it would have to be done with cunning and look like a natural death, but that was second nature to a trained veteran KGB man who had operated in secrecy almost his whole life. As they lay in bed on that fatal final night, Nikolai sat astride the subjugated John Cartwright in sexual embrace and injected the prepared syringe of nothing but air directly into his heart, holding him firmly until he was sure he had died.

It had not been difficult for Nikolai to extricate himself from John's house in Ashdown. The neighbours didn't seem to know he was there, and although John's sister probably did, the local police weren't interested in finding a "missing" lodger once John Cartwright had been declared dead from natural causes, i.e., a heart attack.

It meant that Nikolai Volkov needed to leave the Ashfield area for a while, but Stephen Lodge wasn't there anyway. Of course, Lodge's lady friend was at the cottage quite regularly, mostly at the weekends when an older couple, her parents he assumed, were also there and the opportunity to do the girlfriend any damage without harming others did not present itself. Nikolai wasn't especially bothered about who got hurt in his quest for Pyotr's revenge, but he wasn't stupid either. He knew he had to avoid bringing attention to himself or to his country; his own worst enemies were his KGB bosses who would not think twice about eliminating him if he brought discredit on the Motherland.

NIKOLAI VOLKOV WATCHED as the two lovers walked toward the pyramid building he could see across the way. He wasn't sure what it was, but it did not matter. He had prepared a little treat for them both, but he would need to present it without Lodge identifying him. Nikolai had altered his appearance, but he wasn't that confident it would fool the Englishman. Maybe the girlfriend? When he saw Stephen going off to an ice-cream kiosk leaving Jessica sat on a bench, he saw his opportunity.

"It is a nice day, miss," said Nikolai as he approached the bench, making sure the sun was over his shoulder, blinding Jessica against his true appearance.

"Yes," said Jessica in complete innocence of the older man stood in front of her, "A beautiful summer's day spent in delightful company."

"I must say that you are a beautiful woman who deserves happiness, and your young man there" pointing towards Stephen, "is most fortunate. Might I offer you one of my sweets, a little barley sugar that I always carry with me on a Sunday." And he proffered a bag toward Jessica.

"You are very kind, sir," as she accepted two wrapped sweets placed into her hand. "We are about to have ice cream so would you mind if I kept these for later. We are going swimming at the Pyramid pool and might be glad of them after to rid our mouths of the taste of chlorine."

"You are very welcome," said Nikolai, waving his stick in the air, "But now I must get on and complete my Sunday circular walk. Good exercise for the heart and legs, you see." And with that, he doffed his cap and continued his way across the Common.

"Who was that?" asked Stephen as he returned with two Mr Whippy 99's, with flakes.

"Oh, just some old man enjoying the summer sun," replied Jessica, "as am I." taking one ice-cream from Stephen and giving him a kiss as he sat down on the bench next to her. The two barley sugar sweets had been put into her handbag and Jessica had already forgotten about them.

THE PAIR OF them enjoyed their swim so much that they forgot all about the D-Day Museum, but that didn't matter, another day would do. After their swim, they walked along toward the King's Theatre and found a small restaurant where they could enjoy a good dinner, and then wandered the streets back to HMS Vernon oblivious of anyone and anything other than their own company. Before Jessica left for London, Stephen checked his duty rotation and guaranteed that he could be free for his birthday in two weeks.

"We'll spend the whole weekend in Ashfield," he promised, "and maybe your parents could join us?" He had been dodging Jessica's dad ever since the Eastertime because of the pressure on them to get married. "Why fix what ain't broke," was Stephen and Jessica's constant cry, but her father was never convinced.

"They will be there," chuckled Jessica. "I have already invited them."

Stephen walked her around to the Harbour Station and, after a cuddle and a kiss Jessica boarded what was almost the last train for Waterloo. It had been a good day.

When Jessica had settled herself into her first-class seat, and the guard had checked her ticket, she got her diary out and wrote a few notes for herself. She always enjoyed Stephen's company, loved him like crazy and wished that they could be together always. But he was in the Royal Navy and away so much, and she had her secretarial career at the Foreign Office in London, so they had to make the most of whatever days they could have together. Today had been a good day and, as was her practice, she marked her diary page with a tick. Putting her diary back into her handbag, she spotted the two barley sugar sweets the old man had given her and thought, why not, so she unwrapped one and popped it into her mouth. It tasted ... very ... nice.

"SIR! SIR!" THE Leading Hand of the Watch was trying to wake Stephen up.

"What the ... It can't be morning yet." Stephen's response was stuttering, slow. He was tired and he just couldn't be on duty yet.

"It's three in the morning, sir, and you're wanted on the telephone. The caller says it's urgent!"

"What!" Stephen was suddenly alert. "Who the bloody hell is calling me at three in the morning?"

"The Officer of the Watch has taken the call, sir. He's holding on the line, the caller that is. Sir Geoffrey Cheese or something like that."

"Bloody Hell!" Stephen jumped out of bed wearing just his underwear and a vest. He pulled on his trousers and a white T-shirt while asking the rating where the phone was.

"You can take it in the Wardroom, sir. I'll patch it through." The Leading Hand left Stephen to it and returned to the Guardhouse.

Stephen stumbled downstairs in a hurry. He'd forgotten his standard issue slippers and socks. Barefooted, he ran into the empty Wardroom and found the telephone, which was on a long extension so he could sit himself down.

"Put the call through, Guardhouse," he shouted down the phone as soon as he picked up.

"I'm already through," Sir Geoffrey's voice, strong, alive. "But just listen for a moment and don't interrupt."

"I'm listening, sir," Stephen thought it's got to be

important at three o'clock in the morning. "What the ..."

"Just listen, lad." Sir Geoffrey was very forceful. "This isn't easy to say, so I just need to get it out!"

Stephen was silent.

"It's Jessica! She's been poisoned. She's in a bad way!"

"What!" Stephen jumped to his feet and started pacing up and down. "How? When? Where is she now!?"

"She is at the University College Hospital, London, that's in Euston Road, where I am now. I have already called her parents and they're on their way. I want you to gather up your stuff, money, bankcards, ID, and get yourself to your Guardhouse. I'm sending a couple of Regulators (Royal Navy Police) to Vernon to pick you up and drive you straight to the hospital. I won't say anything more; that would be just a waste of your time and I'd only have to repeat myself when you get here. Make sure you bring everything you need, lad, you could be here a while. And Stephen, remember, it will be worse for her parents!" Sir Geoffrey hung up.

Stephen sat for a while. He couldn't believe what he'd just heard. If it had been anyone else other than Sir Geoffrey, he would have said it had been a very distasteful prank call. But it was Sir Geoffrey and Stephen ran back to his room and quickly got himself into more appropriate clothes, socks, and shoes, filled a small backpack and took his personals:

wallet, bankcards, ID, and ran to the Guardhouse. He hadn't bothered to lock his cabin even though he didn't know how many hours he'd be gone.

The RNPs were waiting for him already and he was on his way within minutes. They drove quickly and quietly through the town but once they hit the A3, they put their blue light on and flew up the road. Stephen sat in the back of their Land Rover, biting on his fingers, and trying to understand what was going on. It was only about seven hours since he said cheerio to Jessica at the railway station, so where had she gone after that? What could have happened that would cause poisoning this serious? Why? How? Who? Stephen realised there had to be someone else involved. It could not be Volkov, could it? The bloody Russian had not surfaced for months. There had been no reports from Ashfield, Ashdown, or anywhere on him or the mysterious tramp that he might have become.

It could not be Volkov! Stephen cried inside. If it were, and if the worst happened, Jessica dying would be on him, Stephen.

WHEN THEY GOT to the hospital, Stephen was directed to a private ward where he found Jessica's parents sat by a bed. Jessica herself was laid out, unmoving and eyes closed, looking drawn and pallid, and covered in tubes and other medical equipment. The monitor showed her heart rate was regular but weak and her blood pressure was extremely low.

Her breathing was supported by wearing an oxygen mask.

Stephen greeted her parents and took hold of Jessica's right hand, giving it an affectionate squeeze. She did not move, but he thought she looked at peace. Seeing Sir Geoffrey through a window to the corridor, he went to talk with him.

"I think the worst has passed, lad, fortunately for Jessica," Sir Geoffrey told him.

"What happened? How did they get in touch with you?" Stephen was tense and could not contain his emotions.

"Jessica called me, about one o'clock this morning. What's that: four hours ago? She's an intelligent girl. She hadn't been able to get hold of you, didn't know where to call I suppose, and she did not want to scare her parents so, she called my personal line and told me she was feeling very unwell. She couldn't stand up for long, had started vomiting, and she was having trouble getting her breath. Guessing that she might have been poisoned, perhaps by some food she ate, I called for an ambulance and asked them to bring her direct to University College."

"But, how?" cried Stephen. "She was with me all day yesterday, and we both ate the same food for dinner. If she has got food poisoning it would have to be something she ate after she caught the train home, and that was late, much later than Jessica would want to eat."

"I don't think this is just normal food poisoning,"

Sir Geoffrey stated. "It's too extreme a reaction for that. I asked the ambulance crew to bring Jessica to University because they have experience here of toxic poisoning, particularly Ricin. It's just a guess, but I and they have history with Ricin. You'll remember Georgi Markov?"

"The Bulgarian who died in 1978?" Stephen was amazed. "Yes. Killed by an injection of Ricin delivered by an umbrella. But that can't have happened to Jessica? There would be no reason?"

"I agree," said Sir Geoffrey, "but this wasn't an injection: it was by ingestion, and Jessica's own quick thinking saved her life. That, and the team here at the hospital, some of whom date back to the Markov case."

"There is something about Ricin poisoning. It seems to suck the air out of you from the inside, almost as if you implode. Inhalation is the worse because that takes the poison straight to the lungs, and then it works its way into other organs and slowly shuts them down. It can take weeks, months even, to kill a person and once it's got a proper hold on the body, there's nothing can be done except palliative care."

"But Jessica is young, and strong, and this was poison by ingestion. Here they very quickly put her on a respirator, pumped her stomach out, and fed her activated charcoal directly into the stomach to counteract the poison – it binds the poison to itself and is then flushed out of the system. What doesn't come out immediately is then usually passed through the normal bodily functions. But, had she not called me and had we not got her in here quickly, within a few more hours it could have been a lot worse. She still has extremely low blood pressure, and her breathing is being supported. I'd say she's over the worst of it, but it will be some days or even weeks before she fully recovers."

Stephen looked into the side ward through the viewing window and watched Jessica's parents sat by her bed, Dad's arm around Mum's back as she held Jessica's hand. He looked at Jessica laid quietly on the bed, her chest rising and falling to the beat of the respirator she was wired up to. Heart monitor cables and other electronic gadgets ran under the blanket covering her body, that gorgeous body that he had enjoyed so often, and would be stuck to her skin at strategic points by those circular pads that you see on televised medical programs. He knew that he loved this woman, who he had been with for more than four years but knew that she had to put up with his long absences when he was on duty for the Royal Navy and Sir Geoffrey Cheeseman, which held Stephen back from making a complete commitment to her. He knew that Jessica was her parents' only daughter, their only child, and they were devoted to her, always on hand to help her out, happy to see her in a firm relationship but happy also to have her at home whenever she would visit them. They were immensely proud of their daughter and excited to think that she might settle down in Dorset at the cottage they had been able to help her redecorate and modernise. Jessica's father looked up to see Stephen who knew he should be by her side as they were now, but he had more questions for Sir Geoffrey first. He acknowledged Dad's look and indicated he would be there in a few minutes.

"But, how?" asked Stephen again. "I'm not any clearer on how or where Jessica would come into contact with Ricin. What's the source, and how could it be administered?"

"Ricin comes from castor beans," Sir Geoffrey told him. "The manufacture of Castor Oil that our parents used to give us for stomach upsets, has revealed that a little Ricin is contained in each bean, balanced out by the greater oil content, but there have been numerous incidents where castor bean factory workers have ingested Ricin simply by sucking on their fingers after sorting the beans. Of course, most of the oil production is done now by machine, and workers have to wear disposable masks as well as rubber gloves, but inhalation can still be a problem."

"If it is administered by injection, as in the Markov case, the Ricin enters the bloodstream directly and is almost always fatal, even though it can still be slow. Inhalation is the most common cause but that would affect many people at once as it's in the air, but that is not the case here. Somehow, Jessica has ingested Ricin through something she's eaten, and

I can't imagine she's been chewing on castor beans to pass the time."

"I can't imagine her eating anything yesterday that I didn't also eat," Stephen was thoughtful. "We were together the whole day, had a snack for lunch and a dinner at a Southsea Indian restaurant. And an ice cream on the Southsea Common before going swimming at the Pyramid pool."

"Jessica's not that big an eater. Likes to keep her figure slim and goes to the gym most days. The only thing she does do, usually after a spicy meal, is that she'll take a peppermint or a boiled sweet to take the taste out of her mouth."

"And did you have spicy food at your dinner?" asked Sir Geoffrey.

"We had curry," replied Stephen, "I had Chicken Korma, and Jessica asked for Dal Makhani, both mild curries.

"Kidney beans," said Sir Geoffrey.

"Kidney beans?" responded Stephen.

"Dal Makhani," Sir Geoffrey knew his Indian food. "Kidney beans are part of the recipe, but I wonder … could a castor bean get mixed in instead. I shall need the address of that restaurant, Stephen. We'll have to do an inspection there just in case."

"But it couldn't be, sir. Jessica was with me until almost ten p.m. and she wasn't showing any signs of illness or feeling sick."

"Ingested Ricin can take it's time, Stephen. If there was a castor bean mixed into that curry, the castor oil would have countered the Ricin for a while but, eventually the Ricin would show itself."

Then Sir Geoffrey asked, "But, what about barley sugar?"

"Barley sugar?" Stephen looked at Sir Geoffrey, wondering what he would say next. "Where does barley sugar come into it?"

"Well, you said that Jessica likes a mint or a boiled sweet after a spicy meal. I rummaged through her handbag when they brought her in and found a barley sugar sweet, two actually, one still wrapped, and one empty wrapper. Which would suggest to me that she had eaten a sweet recently, on the train coming home."

"I've never known her to eat a barley sugar," queried Stephen, more to himself than anyone. "I've never known her to even buy them; they're a bit old fashioned aren't they? The sort of sweet given out on a short plane flight maybe, if you don't have Fruit Bon Bon's, that is." Stephen was remembering his own flight down from Edinburgh recently, and then recalled Jessica's own flight for her birthday. "It's possible she got those on her Edinburgh flights when she visited me in November last year."

"I'm going to get the sweet forensically evaluated anyway. No stone unturned," said Sir Geoffrey. "And you'd best get back in there," indicating Jessica's private ward, "and comfort the parents while I organise that test. Please, report to my office when you can later this morning."

"Aye, aye, sir," Stephen responded with a handshake, and went back in to sit at Jessica's bedside.

BY ELEVEN O'CLOCK, Jessica's blood pressure had turned a corner and was coming up again. Her heart rate was stronger, and the doctors reckoned she was past the worse, thank God. She was still unconscious though, and Mum and Dad stayed with her while Stephen excused himself so he could report back to Sir Geoffrey.

"It's confirmed, Stephen," said Sir Geoffrey the moment Stephen arrived at his office. "Toxicology is just in, and their report confirms Ricin. Nothing on the spare wrapper but enough in the uneaten sweet to give one a really bad stomach-ache and rip the other organs apart in a few days if it's not picked up straight away."

"But, where did the barley sugar come from, sir? Jessica can't have had those in her handbag these past eight months without at least trying one." Stephen was baffled.

"I've no idea," Sir Geoffrey told him, "I reckon the only person who can is Jessica herself, and until she regains consciousness we can't even talk to her. We will have to be patient, my boy; until then, I want you to go back to the hospital and stay as long as you can. You have access to Jessica's flat so her parents can use that as their base, but I want you to wait at the hospital day and night until Jessica is awake and able to talk."

Stephen accepted the task given to him without question and with fortitude. He agreed with Sir Geoffrey that the parents should not suspect anything deliberate about Jessica's poisoning but be reassured that Sir Geoffrey's department were looking into the causes of it.

JOHNNY "JACK" JOHNSTON was miserable. The old faggot was going to lose his lodger of the last two months and wondered how he was going to cope through the summer. He had met the man in the Lion Terrace cottage late one night and had taken him back to his house when he found out the man was homeless. They'd come to an arrangement when the Russian, who couldn't give much money for lodgings had agreed to share Jack's bed, and it had been a pleasurable relationship.

Ex-Royal Navy seaman Johnny Jack knew he was past his best, but still liked to stalk the Pompey cottages, picking up the occasional young matelot who was too drunk to go back to their ship or barracks, and too drunk to care where they slept. He was born in Dumbarton, Scotland, and had served a full term of twenty-four years with the Andrew as it was called after Andrew Miller who pressganged recruits onto ships during the French Revolutionary and Napoleonic Wars. After he was discharged he decided to settle in Portsmouth where he bought a small, terraced house in Britannia Road, not far from Fratton Station, and worked for the council as a Museum assistant.

Portsmouth had changed greatly over the years, not necessarily for the better in Jack's opinion as he bemoaned the reduction in service personnel based in the town, Navy ratings especially. Jack was nearer seventy now, too old, and too poor to move on anywhere else. When Nikolai, the Russian, was gone, he would have to endure another summer on his own and he did not look forward to it.

"Do you have to leave so soon?" Jack asked his lodger as they sat down to dinner that Sunday evening.

"I am afraid so, old man," replied Nikolai Volkov. "My money is running out and I have seen enough of Portsmouth. I need to return home to the motherland and find work."

"You could find work here," said Jack, trying to be optimistic. "There must be something you can do, being so knowledgeable about the world as you are. There are opportunities coming up as the University starts to expand, and the museums always need staff."

"I do not have the right work permits though, do I. We have had this conversation before, and I have to return to my own country to apply for a new visa. No, old man, I have to leave soon, but it has been good, and I have to thank you for the use of your clothes, and your hospitality. Very pleasurable, no?"

Jack was still intrigued by this stranger who had come into his life at the beginning of May. Having picked up the Russian in the Lion Terrace public toilets and offering him a home when Nikolai had nowhere else to go, he was surprised by how smartly dressed the man became in Jack's own clothes which he could no longer wear, and how clever he was, and wondered why he was homeless. But, he had enjoyed having someone to share his bed with and they had occasionally gone out and trawled the streets together. He found Nikolai to be entertaining, and sexy. Even an old faggot like Jack had needs, and Nikolai readily satisfied his.

"Why not take in a student or two," Nikolai suggested. "There must be plenty about looking for cheap lodgings. A couple of girls perhaps; no danger to you, and I am sure they would be safe from you. You could move into the front room down here, I can help with that, and the two bedrooms upstairs can be made good for your lodgers."

"It's an idea, I suppose," Jack responded, "but I'd rather have young lads than girls."

"And I know why, you old bugger. But that would just get you into trouble. You have to accept, old man, that your best chance for companionship is with people like me, middle-aged, and not particularly caring who they sleep with."

Jack let the offensive remark pass over his head. "How will you get home to Russia if your money is running out. I can't help you, I'm sorry to say."

Nikolai took an envelope from the inside pocket of the green tweed he was still wearing. "I have an open return ticket for a flight to Moscow. It is valid for one year from last August. I have to use it while I still can, another reason why I need to go now."

Jack knew when he was beaten, so he looked forward with quiet resignation to their last few nights together. Nikolai told him he had arranged a flight from London Gatwick for the following weekend, which he could get to cheaply and directly by train and assembled the few belongings that he had into a small, scruffy, backpack, so he'd be ready to go.

He spent every morning poring over the local paper as if he were expecting an article to appear.

"What are you looking for in that paper, Nikolai? You seem more interested this week than any time before."

The Russian thought how he could reply without being dishonest.

"I saw a couple on Southsea Common on Sunday, and I thought they were a celebrity couple that I had seen on the television or somewhere. She was unbelievably beautiful, and the man was quite handsome too, and I wondered what they were doing in town. I thought, maybe if there is a new show coming to the King's Theatre, I could confirm I was right about them. But I have not seen anything in the paper."

"And you probably won't," said Jack, "I never find the local rag is up to date. But there is a new Summer Show coming in August so, you might be right."

What Nikolai was really looking for was a

report on two locals being admitted to hospital with serious poisoning. He hoped at least to read about the beautiful woman's death, but he was to be disappointed.

THE BEAUTIFUL WOMAN in question was lying unconscious in the University College Hospital in London, where she was slowly recovering from Ricin poisoning. Her boyfriend, Stephen, stayed at the hospital for four nights before Jessica woke up. The hospital staff had offered him a private room, paid for by the MoD, but he stayed at Jessica's bedside by night and only slept briefly during the daytime when her parents came to relieve him from his vigil.

Stephen telephoned Sir Geoffrey Cheeseman's office on Friday morning and spoke to his secretary, Hazel Eaves. "She's awake, Hazel!" Stephen spoke excitedly. "Jessica's awake! Can you please tell Sir Geoffrey. I need to get back to her bedside."

"That's great news, Stephen," Hazel was on her feet already. "Such a relief. I'll tell Sir Geoffrey straight away. He'll probably want to come up there, but if not, he'll surely telephone the hospital."

Stephen returned to her bedside, where Jessica's parents were looking relieved and tearful at the same time, still worried about their daughter's weakened condition. Doctors and nurses were fussing around Jessica but not pushing her family away and Stephen, with Mum and Dad, sat quietly waiting to talk with the patient. Time seemed to be standing still but Sir Geoffrey turned up within the hour and spoke with all of them.

When the doctors had given them clearance and Jessica's parents had gone to the hospital canteen for a cup of tea, both Stephen and Sir Geoffrey tried to get Jessica to talk to them, but she was clearly struggling and slipped into unconsciousness.

"All we need to know really," said Sir Geoffrey to Stephen in particular, "is how she came to be in possession of those barley sugar sweets and how long she'd had them?"

"I agree," Stephen responded, "but it looks like it will be another day or two before she's well enough to talk, and I don't want to push it."

"You've probably realised, Stephen" Sir Geoffrey continued, "that I've pulled you out of your Naval duties, so time is not a problem there. But we do need to solve this one, and sooner rather than later."

"Yes, I know," said Stephen, "but I do not want Jessica stressed trying to remember how those sweets got in her bag while she is still as weak as she is."

"You really care about this woman, Stephen." It was as if Sir Geoffrey was realising his employee's love for Jessica for the first time.

"Yes, I do." Stephen was almost in tears.

"Perhaps you should tell her how you really feel," advised Sir Geoffrey. "Before you lose her. Life will be different for Jessica after this incident. She might prefer the comforts of her parents' home to waiting for you to pop the question and marry her."

"Women can be contrary, Stephen. I gave up trying to work out Sarah, Lady Cheeseman, years ago, and she has never disappointed me. But I do know she nearly gave up on my dithering and dallying while I got posted to here, there, and everywhere, during my Army days. They won't wait forever while us men get inside their head and decide a service life is not for them."

"I hear what you're saying, Sir Geoffrey, but I don't know what my future service life will be like. I could be away at sea all the time for all I know."

"But that is what I'm saying, Stephen." Sir Geoffrey pressed his point. "You're making the choice for Jessica. You're deciding what she will say if she could choose for herself. I'll always remember my good lady very loudly asking me over a dinner we shared in a public restaurant, when I was going to make an honest woman of her. I was just about to be posted to Germany – this was post-World War II – for nine months and she said, 'So what, I can live in married quarters, can't I?' So, we got married quickly in a registry office and we've never looked back since."

Stephen knew that Sir Geoffrey had a point, and he would love nothing more than to settle down with Jessica. The pair of them knew how they felt about each other but there was a lingering shadow over their long-term future while Stephen served out his time in the Royal Navy. He thought of it as a risk, but perhaps a risk worth taking. It was Jessica's decision as well to make.

And it would make her dad happy too.

IT WAS ABOUT nine p.m. when Stephen felt Jessica squeeze his hand. He had dozed at her bedside but quickly came awake when she responded to his hand holding hers. Her parents had gone home for the night and Sir Geoffrey had returned to his office hours before, so Stephen and Jessica were alone. She was still wired up to a heart monitor but no longer wore a mask or had intravenous tubes running through her nose, so he leant across and kissed her. She smiled, eyes open, and he looked at her with love and thankfulness.

"What happened?" she whispered. "And where am I?" She tried to look around but was still too weak to move much.

Stephen told her what hospital she was in and how long she had been there. He told her that her parents were staying in her London flat and would be back in in the morning, but they had been by her bedside every day, as had he, and night-times too. He asked her if she could remember any of what had happened and Jessica shook her head.

"The only thing I remember is waking up in my bed in the early hours after seeing you on Sunday and feeling nauseous and trying to catch my breath. My chest hurt and I telephoned Sir Geoffrey to try and get help."

"Why didn't you just phone for an ambulance?" asked Stephen.

"I needed to let you know where I was, and I was getting worse. I couldn't get through to you and I knew if I got hold of Sir Geoffrey, he would then tell you. And then I collapsed, and I guess you know more about what's happened since than I do."

"I don't even know what has been wrong with me!" Jessica questioned as loudly as she could.

"We do," said Stephen, now sat on the bed and holding both her hands tightly. "You were poisoned ... with Ricin."

"Ricin!" Jessica tried to raise her head and failed. "But that's...?"

"Really bad stuff, yes, we know. But you saved yourself by getting in touch with Sir Geoffrey so soon. And he had you brought here, to University College Hospital, because they have history with this kind of thing."

"And because of their quick action," continued Stephen before she could interrupt him, "you are thankfully still with us today." He leant forward and kissed her again.

"But how?" Jessica asked. "And when?"

"The when is easy," said Stephen. "Either when we were together on Sunday evening, or on the train going home."

"The how we can't be certain, but," he spoke circumspectly, "do you know anything about Barley Sugar sweets?"

"Barley Sugar?" Jessica was confused.

"Yes. Two sweets, well, one sweet uneaten and

one wrapper were found in your handbag..."

"You went through my handbag!" said Jessica, alarmed.

"I didn't, but Sir Geoffrey did," Stephen smiled because now he was sure that Jessica would recover. "Anyway, two barley sugar sweets, which I thought you might have got on your flight back from Edinburgh last November, were found in your handbag. Do you remember where they came from or how long they had been there? They are the source of your Ricin intake."

"Barley sugar," Jessica repeated, wistfully. "No, I don't know. I'm so confused, but I don't think they came from my Caledonian flight. No, wait! The old man on the Common!"

"The Common?" said Stephen, himself confused now.

"Southsea Common ... on Sunday when you went for an ice cream. The old man who spoke to me, and you asked who he was when you came back."

Stephen remembered now. "Green tweed. Walking stick?"

"Yes, that's right," Jessica was flushed with excitement. "He spoke very nicely to me and gave me two barley sugar sweets, one for you and one for me. But we were about to have ice cream and go for a swim and then I placed them in my handbag and forgot about them. Until later, when I was sat on the train, and I could still taste curry in my mouth so I ..." She trailed off, a scared look on her face.

"So you sucked on a barley sugar," said Stephen. "Thank God you did not have the other one as well, otherwise you would not be here! But, tell me about this man. What age would you say he was? Did he speak well, posh like?"

"He would be about the age of my dad. He spoke good English, but with the slightest of accents."

"Bearded, bespectacled? Long-haired?"

"No beard. Grey hair under a flat cap, not especially long. Glasses, yes, heavy rimmed but ordinary lenses.

"As soon as you are able, Sir Geoffrey will get a sketch artist with an ID kit to come and you can build a composite together," said Stephen. "And then I'm going to have to take it back to Harri Jasper and see if she can identify that person. I think you might have just found our tramp!"

EARLY SATURDAY MORNING, and the tramp was saying goodbye to Johnny Jack Johnston. Between them, they had moved Jack's bed and wardrobe downstairs to the front room and turned the upstairs rooms into single bedsits. An advert had been placed in the local paper and on the notice board of Portsmouth Polytechnic. Nikolai took a small paper bag from his pocket.

"Something to remember me by," he said gaily. "Not many left so, don't eat them all at once" He gave the old man an affectionate hug and was gone.

The bag with just a few barley sugar sweets sat on the hall table.

Chapter 9

Return to Ashfield

STEPHEN LODGE HAD managed to contact Sir Geoffrey Cheeseman on his personal line late on Friday night. Sir Geoffrey was home for the weekend and thinking of spending a summery July Saturday playing golf but, duty first, and he headed into town early for a meeting with Stephen at the University College Hospital.

Jessica's parents were back by her bedside having been called by Stephen the night before and were thankful to find her awake and getting stronger all the while, although still confined to bed. Sir Geoffrey talked with her briefly and agreed with Stephen's request for an ID-sketch artist to come in and work with Jessica for a description of the man she had met on Southsea Common. But that would not happen until Monday.

"Can we afford the time to wait, Stephen?" asked Sir Geoffrey. "Should we not start looking straightway?"

"But where, sir? All we do know is that this man, whoever he was but I am guessing on Nikolai Volkov, was on Southsea Common last Sunday. And that was six days ago!"

"But it gives us a starting point," said Sir Geoffrey. "I'll put a call out to keep watch on all the Portsmouth railway stations, and the bus station at the Hard, and pull the CCTV from them since last Sunday."

"Don't forget to include Fratton, sir. All trains stop there as well."

"I'll get onto it straightaway. In the meantime, I am going to have to separate you from your girlfriend and send you back to Portsmouth. The Navy will need something of an explanation about your absence."

Stephen was about to raise a protest, but Sir Geoffrey stopped him.

"It won't be a problem, lad, but you'll have to be excused duties until this business is complete and you're new to the Portsmouth team, so they deserve a bit of a fill-in. Only to the officers, mind, and I need to be sure the door stays open on your Warfare training opportunity."

"And possible promotion," Stephen smiled. "I had guessed you were behind that, sir."

"Actually not," said Sir Geoffrey, "although there is benefit to both of us if your capable talents get sharpened up. No, the recommendation for promotion comes from your last skipper, Lt Commander Duncan Robson, and the Warfare Officers Training Course is a necessary step towards that."

"For the moment," Stephen looked urgently at Sir Geoffrey, "all I want to do is see Jessica get better and find whoever did this to her and bring them to book!"

"And we will, lad. And we will."

NIKOLAI BOARDED THE train at Fratton. The Great Western (Wessex) train was headed for Cardiff via Southampton, Salisbury, Bath, and Bristol. For a Saturday, it was quiet at the station but the train itself, which started at the Harbour was quite busy and he was lucky to get a seat. No First-Class ticket for Nikolai, even though they were on sale he couldn't afford it, but these two-car Sprinters were single-class anyway and anyone riding one with a First-Class ticket would be disappointed and have to claim back from British Rail, a process that usually took months.

Although he'd bought a ticket on a cheap deal for Exeter St David's, Nikolai was intending to get off at Sherborne, so he changed trains at Salisbury. While there was a risk of being spotted he had unfinished business at Ashfield where he sought revenge on Roy Jasper who had prevented him from killing Stephen Lodge twenty months before.

Volkov still hoped to read news of Stephen Lodge and his girlfriend's deaths in Portsmouth, but he couldn't wait there forever. The old faggot, Johnny Jack Johnston, had served his purpose and Nikolai had left that bag of barley sugar sweets expecting Jack to succumb to the Ricin contained in one of them. He didn't want to run the risk of Jack getting chatty with the local law should they come looking. And they would, Nikolai acknowledged that. There would be witnesses that would have seen him on Southsea Common "where a young couple were fatally poisoned." At least, that's what he expected to see in the newspapers, and he thought news like that would get into the national press.

No, he would become as he did before, a tramp passing through the country village of Ashfield. He was not worried about the local bobbies. Nikolai was confident John Cartwright's death would have been recorded as a heart attack brought on by his obesity. The thought of the fat Englishman whose needs he'd had to satisfy for so long left a bitter memory. Johnny Jack had been far simpler, far less demanding.

STEPHEN LODGE ARRIVED back in HMS Vernon, also by train, before noon on Saturday. The Guardhouse had been advised of his return and he was relieved to see that his white Viva SL was still parked where he'd left it. He was told by the Leading Hand of the duty watch to report directly to the Captain's office "where the Skipper's waiting to receive you, sir." Best get this over with, thought Stephen.

Captain Jonathan Husband was not best pleased with being recalled to his office on a Saturday. He liked his weekends, spending time with his family, going to Sunday Mass at St John's Catholic Cathedral in Edinburgh Road, and he enjoyed the relaxed life of a nine-to-five, five-day-week sailor, which he thought he deserved.

"Lieutenant Lodge," he began, "you need to tell me the reason for your absence this week. I know about your girlfriend, so you can spare me some of the details, but there is more to this, I'll wager."

Stephen had to think how he could answer the Captain's questions without giving away the work he did for the Ministry of Defence and Sir Geoffrey.

"You know that my 'girlfriend' was poisoned, sir?"

"Yes. And I am told that Ricin was used and that's not something you can pick up easily on the street." Captain Husband was aware of Jessica's situation, having been briefed by his senior, Captain Brian Moss, from HMS Nelson. "But what's behind it all?"

Stephen decided to be truthful but to tell only half a story.

"A couple of years ago, late 1982, I was targeted by a Russian KGB agent who I must have picked up as an illegal immigrant to the country while on coastal patrol. That was my job then. He escaped and tried to kill me but instead killed my landlady, an eighty-five-year-old resident in a country village in Dorset. I managed to catch up with him and he was arrested and sent down for his crime but, as these things do, he was exchanged last August for two of our own agents and returned to Russia."

Captain Husband sat quietly, listening intently.

"So now, it seems that he has come back to finish the job but, instead of me, he managed to poison

Jessica, my girlfriend, who is getting better by the day, thank God."

"And he will target you again, no doubt," said the Captain. "And if you stay here, that puts us all at risk?"

"On base here? No, I don't think any of us have anything to fear here, but I do need to find this man and I cannot do that by staying at HMS Vernon."

"And so, I have to release you from your duties?" the captain looked at Stephen, raising a hand to stop any interruption. "Oh, don't worry, I haven't been given much choice, and it's bloody inconvenient but, orders are orders, Mr Lodge, as you well know. So, before the end of today, you will clear out your locker and shut up your cabin and leave the key at the Guardhouse on your way to leaving my ship."

"But I would like to return, sir?" Stephen was concerned at his commanding officer's hostility. "As soon as I've dealt with this business. I like it here. Teaching those youngsters, attending the Warfare training..."

"And getting your promotion, no doubt!" interrupted Captain Husband. "We shall have to see what happens. That's not my decision either. But, if I had the choice, I would not have you back as a part-time employee. I need someone who can put their heart into the teaching role full-time and commit for the next one or two years."

"With respect, sir," Stephen was compelled to defend himself. "I didn't want this to happen either. I did not expect my girlfriend to become a target."

"But you knew that *you* might?" Captain Husband was ahead of Stephen. "And I am told you are the only one that can deal with this man, this enemy of yours. What special talent sets you apart from the rest of us? I want to see you progress, Mr Lodge. I would be quite happy for you to be promoted, and I am told that your students, this year's recruits, are enjoying your practical methods when teaching them, and that's a rare thing."

"And now, I have to let you go, and ask someone junior to you and less experienced to step in and finish off the last few weeks of term. I am not happy with that, but I have no choice!"

"I'm very sorry..."

"Spare me the apology, Lieutenant," the Captain interrupted again, red-faced, and keen to go home. "Just do what I said for today, and, if you return to my command, I shall hope for a better attendance from you."

Stephen was dismissed from the Captain's office and went to his cabin to pack.

NIKOLAI ARRIVED AT Sherborne and reckoned he would be able to hitch a ride to Ashfield fairly easily, but there was no rush. The Russian did not want to arrive in Ashfield until the evening, so he took a walk around the town of Sherborne. He was glad of the freedom, to be somewhere where no one would know him or would be looking for him, and where he could relax.

Sherborne is an attractive market town with about nine thousand residents. Located on the main A30 road which stretched from London to Penzance, it is a popular stopover for travellers making that journey. The river Yeo ran alongside the town, and it was noted by ramblers for the hiking routes across the nearby Blackmore Vale and North Dorset Downs. Many of the older properties, including the Abbey Church of St Mary the Virgin, are built of honey-coloured ham stone, and Sherborne Castle, a 16th Century mansion built by the explorer, Sir Walter Raleigh, with gardens designed by the landscape architect, Capability Brown, remains standing.

Nikolai decided in the end to take the last afternoon bus that was going to Ashfield. He knew the bus would call into villages along the way and sat at the back dozing as he travelled the seventy minutes it took to make the journey. He got off the bus before it got into the village proper and walked the rest of the way. He kept himself out of sight as much as he could, covering his face with the bonnet of his coat whenever the occasional car drove past on Haywards Lane. It didn't take long to reach Ashfield Primary School where he could watch the pub from the obscurity of an alleyway to one side.

Volkov knew from past observations that Roy Jasper always went to the Greene Dragon on a Saturday evening for a few hours and wished he'd done this job before. It would have saved the risk of returning to Ashfield. But he knew that he could not expose his presence before Lodge was dealt with and he believed that was now. Nikolai waited and sure enough, Roy entered the pub alone at about seven-thirty p.m. He also knew that Roy was a creature of habit and would be there for just ninety minutes, so he remained vigilant.

"HAPPY TO SEE you, Roy," said Tiny Tim as Roy Jasper walked into his public bar. "The usual?"

"Yes please, Tim" Roy answered. "A pint of Huntsman's would go down a treat."

"Trouble at home?" queried Tim.

"No, not especially. Harri is still a bit fractious, but it's been a tough two years for her. And Sheila's finding it difficult to concentrate on the shop work once Harri's home from school."

"Aah well," said Tim, "It's been tough for all of you after that kidnapping incident. But you're still the hero from that time, aren't you, and being at home for longer must help?"

Roy knew they'd had this conversation many times since he, Roy, saved the lives of his daughter and Stephen Lodge from the Russian agents. But he was always grateful for a sympathetic ear, and since the death of her teacher and Harri's continued insistence that he was killed, despite the inquest verdict that Mr John Cartwright died from a heart attack, life at home was strained. So Roy was glad to get to the pub on a weekend and drown his thoughts with a few beers before returning to another week of office work. Sheila never came up with him, preferring a bottle of wine at home, and that suited Roy, he could leave his wife to look after their rather excitable and fanciful nine-year-old daughter.

"Any news from the Lodge?" as Stephen had become known, Tim asked.

"No, nothing at all," replied Roy, "and we haven't seen Jessica for a couple of weeks either. That's unusual in itself."

"I do miss that woman," mused Tim, "more than I do Stephen."

"You're still fancying the pants off her, you sly dog," chuckled Roy. "You haven't got a chance, you know that, don't you? I haven't seen a girl so besotted with her man since Sheila first caught sight of me."

The two men laughed.

"Aah well," Tim made to go off and serve some other customers. "The better man loses. I'll keep wishing until it's too late or they get married or something."

Roy finished his first pint and asked for another. He thought about a game of darts, but no one seemed interested, so he found a newspaper and sat in a corner to have a read. The news was dominated by the latest on the Miner's Strike, which was really beginning to get nasty. The fallout was continuing from the Battle of Orgreave in mid-June. Roy recalled watching it on the late-night TV news: six thousand police against five thousand picketing miners and their women, it was the ugliest thing Roy had ever witnessed on British soil. He sympathised with the miners who were losing their jobs, and their communities in some cases, but knew that Arthur Scargill and the NUM had talked them into strike action without holding any kind of ballot. Margaret Thatcher's government were planning to change the rules on legal strikes.

Roy stuck it out for another hour and another pint of Huntsman's ale and left the pub to walk back home just after nine o'clock. The sun was setting and the streetlights, of which there were precious few, had come on while Roy was in the Greene Dragon, but he did not see the hooded figure of Nikolai Volkov steal across the street from his hiding place. Roy was halfway home when he was assaulted from behind, Volkov's left arm wrapping around his neck and the sharp point of a knife being rammed into his lower back. Roy cried out in fear and pain and tried to turn around to face his attacker, but Volkov held him firm and dragged him noisily down a pathway between two houses. The knife, a short-bladed fisherman's folding knife that had once belonged to Volkov's father had already entered Roy's right side and when it was dark enough for Volkov's face not to be recognised, the Russian pushed his victim against the house wall and leant in close so that he could talk to him.

"Well, my friend, we meet again, only this time I am in charge!" he said, quietly but with menace.

Roy recognised the voice straightaway but could not respond. Volkov's arm smothered his mouth, and he was slipping into unconsciousness.

"You should have let me complete my task the last time, Mr Jasper. Maybe your daughter would have survived, but I would have had my revenge on Stephen Lodge. And now, you must die instead." Volkov pushed and twisted the short blade, piercing a kidney, then pulled Roy around, slipping his sharpened knife around to the front. Jasper's body was already limp as it slid down the wall. Nikolai lifted the knife to Roy's throat, but a light suddenly shone down the darkened alleyway.

"Hey! What's going on here!" a voice cried out. A resident from the house on one side of the path had heard a commotion and thought it might be a fox in a dustbin. He shone his torch down the pathway that separated him from his neighbour's house and saw two shadowy figures on the ground. The light from his torch reflected back from what he saw was a knife blade and he shouted a warning. The one with the knife, disguised by a hood, rose to his feet, and ran down the pathway, scrambling over the neighbour's gate when he got to the blocked end. The other person stayed lying on the ground and seemed to be unable to move.

"Mavis!" the resident called indoors. "Call for an ambulance! We've got an injured person out here." The resident, too old to climb over his fence, ran around his front gate and came down the pathway where he found Roy unconscious and bleeding badly from a stab wound to the back. Ex-ambulance driver and retiree, Ted, placed a big hand around the knife wound and pressed in to try and stop the bleeding. He prayed for the ambulance to hurry up or they were going to lose this man, who he recognised as the part-owner of Jasper's down the road. His wife, Mavis, came out and told Ted the ambulance was on its way, and she had also called the police who had to come from Ashdown. Ted knew the nearest hospital was Yeatman at Sherborne, but he expected an ambulance to come up from Wimborne Minster; it was not really nearer but was a quicker drive when you're in a hurry.

The Ashdown police turned up first. Police-Sergeant Ronald Blake and his two constables had turned out at the first call and took over from Ted and Mavis in dealing with Roy Jasper. They ripped Roy's jacket off from his body and one of the constables who was a first aider asked Mavis for some long strips of cotton sheeting. Country dwellers are practical folk and she very quickly turned out a white sheet which she cut and ripped, and the constable who had been applying pressure to Roy's wound, placed a wad of material over it and bound it in place with the cut sheets. Mavis had also brought out a blanket which they used to keep Roy warm.

The commotion had attracted a crowd by now, including Sheila Jasper who was standing down by the General Store. She could not join the throng because Harri was asleep in her bed, but she continued to watch. An ambulance crew arrived to take over from the police, and an assessment of Roy's condition told them he would have to go to a hospital as quickly as possible. Yeatman was the nearest but didn't deal with this kind of wound so it would have to be the Dorset County Hospital at Dorchester and that was quite far. Sergeant Blake called a contact in the Royal Corps of Signals barracks at Blandford Forum and asked for their help with a serious stab-wound victim from Ashfield, but they said it would be quicker to take Roy across Tolworth Down and direct to the Dorset, and the ambulance crew agreed.

NIKOLAI VOLKOV HAD escaped by climbing the neighbour's garden gate but then had to climb more fences as he made his way across other gardens, waking up at least two dogs who barked loudly until lights were turning on in nearby houses and cottages. He managed to get out onto a road and made his way quickly toward the Downs. He remembered well enough the area around the village but knew if he were going to get right away he would need a vehicle of some sort, so he resolved to stealing a car. He made his way to Fennel Farm on Ashfield Hill and very quickly found what he wanted there. He easily hot-wired an old Datsun Cherry belonging to the farmer, Tom Walker, and quietly and smoothly drove out of the farm gate and turned left up Ashfield Hill. No lights had come on at the farm and no dogs.

Nikolai counted his Russian chickens! As he drove up the hill, an ambulance with flashing blue lights but no siren dashed past him and into the village. He cursed and hoped that, if it were for Mr Jasper, they would be too late.

STEPHEN LODGE ARRIVED on his driveway just before ten-thirty p.m., still wearing his regulation No 2 uniform, a requirement when officially leaving a naval base. He had not hurried from HMS Vernon, wanting first to telephone and check on Jessica's progress. She was still unable to take the call herself, but her father said that she was comfortable and stable, and getting stronger.

He saw Sheila stood outside the Store as he swung around the corner and could see blue lights flashing a couple of hundred yards up the street. He ran up to the Store from Farthing Corner House to where Sheila was standing just in time to see an ambulance speeding away from the scene.

"What's going on, Sheila?" he asked.

"I don't know, Stephen," Sheila replied. "Thank goodness you are home, but I wish Roy were here. He went up to the 'Dragon earlier and he's normally back long before now. Harri's in bed so I can't leave the Store."

"I'll run up there and see what I can do," said Stephen, and he was gone before Sheila could say anymore.

THE FIRST PERSON he recognised was Police Sergeant Blake and he knew it was bad by the way the constables were keeping folk out of their "crime scene."

"I haven't seen you in a while, Sergeant," said Stephen.

"And neither have I you, Mr Lodge, but you always seem to turn up like a bad penny when someone's been murdered, or an attempt has been made." The police sergeant and Stephen had history. "You'll be telling me next the Special Branch are on their way."

"No, but it wouldn't surprise me if they did turn up. They're not that far away actually, just down in Blandford where they've been for the last two months or so. I'm surprised they haven't popped into your constabulary to say hi."

"But enough about us," Stephen said hastily. "What's going on here?"

"A man has been stabbed! He's not been formally identified yet but, informally, Ted Jarvis here," waving his hand at the elderly rescuer, "says it's Roy Jasper from the local store."

"What? Roy. How?" Stephen said too loudly.

"Clearly, the 'how' is with a knife," Sergeant Blake was characteristically facetious. "As to the rest, our investigations are only just starting, Mr Lodge, and I must get on. I take it you'll go back to the Store so, perhaps, you could check if Roy Jasper is there."

"I know that he's not," Stephen had faced annoyance at Police-Sergeant Blake before. "I've just spoken with Sheila, and she tells me she is still waiting for Roy to come home from the pub."

"Then I'd better come down with you. I can leave my constables here guarding the crime scene and waiting on Forensics, while we go to see Mrs Jasper and give her what news we can."

Stephen and Sergeant Blake walked briskly down the street to Sheila's store and gestured her inside, asking her to take a seat.

"A man has been badly injured with a knife, Mrs Jasper," the policeman didn't beat about the bush. "It might be your husband!"

Sheila screamed and Stephen could hear tiny feet running around upstairs. He knew Harri would be down within seconds.

"Where is this man that you say has been stabbed?" asked Sheila as Harri ran into the store and up to her mother.

"He's being taken to the Dorset County Hospital in Dorchester. He's lost a lot of blood and he's in a bad way and will have to undergo emergency surgery. Let's hope we are in time, but I need either you or Lieutenant Lodge here to come with me and identify our victim, alive or not."

Harri burst into tears, joining her mother who had been crying the whole time.

"You're not very good with sensitive issues, are you, Sergeant." Stephen spoke sternly. "I think Sheila will have to go with one of your constables, while you cover investigations at the crime scene.

And I will look after Harri." He concluded, looking at Sheila and Harri.

"I want to go with Mummy," Harri looked back at him.

"Not this time, Harri," Stephen was firm. "The kind of hospital that Mummy has to go to doesn't want us extras to be getting in the way. If it is your dad, Mummy can telephone us, and we can see about going down tomorrow. If that's okay with Mummy, of course?"

Sheila didn't know what to say. She was in shock from the news and could only sit there and look at them all.

"Come on, Mrs Jasper," said the police sergeant. "Put a coat on, and we'll get you on your way."

Harri was going to continue her protest but one look from Stephen shut her up. "All right," she sulked, "I'll stay with Stephen."

SHEILA AND POLICE Sergeant Blake left the Store to walk back up the road so that one of the constables could drive her to Dorchester.

Chapter 10

Chasing shadows

NIKOLAI VOLKOV DIDN'T really know where to go next. He drove the farmer's car up Ashfield Hill and over Tolworth Down, stopping near the church for a time while he gave it some thought. His clothes were stained from the attack on Jasper and while he could change his shirt and trousers, he could not do much with his coat, which was stained with blood. He remembered some of the roads from when he and Dmitri Mikhailov were here but not well enough to plan an escape route that would take him down to the coast. He did not think he could go back to the Embassy in London because, as this was an unsanctioned mission, they would not be impressed by what he had done. In fact, he thought the KGB would just throw him to the wolves!

But Nikolai had been living this life long enough to know how to survive in "enemy territory" as he thought of England. He didn't have access to unlimited funds, but that was not unusual; he could steal what he needed. He was carrying a handgun and a small amount of ammunition along with a few clothes in his backpack. He had his father's knife, of course, which would need to be cleaned off as soon as he could find somewhere suitable. Eventually he would need to buy petrol for the Datsun car, but he wanted to keep off the main roads. His obsession with ridding his world of Pyotr Petrovich's killer, Stephen Lodge, had become too great for him to turn away now, and he knew he would have to find out somehow that Lodge was actually dead. That meant going somewhere where he could access newspapers and a radio, but once he got confirmation, he thought he could find a boat to take him across the Channel and he would make his way through Europe and then home. Volkov was trained to work covertly and was expert in doing so.

Of course, there was a radio in the car, he realised. He wasn't used to that, no disrespect to the Lada car he drove back home. There was also a glove compartment and, as he rummaged through this he found a road map. Not of the whole country but enough of Southern England that he thought he could make his way west or south without using too many main roads. Things were looking up already and Volkov mapped his journey down North Street, which he was on now, and through the village of Winterborne Stickland until he could turn right onto Dunbury Lane. It was not yet midnight and he would need to find somewhere to pull off the road and rest before daylight, so he thought the country lanes would give him the best chance for that. He realised he would also need food and that would be more difficult. There was nowhere open this late at night.

STEPHEN'S HEAD WAS reeling. Everything was happening so fast, and this next week looked as if it would be as bad as the last with Jessica still in hospital, now Roy, and Harri, who was curled up with him on the new two-seater sofa beneath the kitchen hatch, traumatised by the whole business. The poor kid would be a long time getting over this.

Could it all be Volkov? There was no concrete evidence to say it was, no witnesses that could identify Roy's attacker, and he was waiting for what he expected to be the less than useful CCTV footage being retrieved from the Portsmouth train stations. But it was the only conclusion that made sense. Six days of video would take a lot of trawling through so that wouldn't be available quickly. And why would Volkov come back to Ashfield again? If he'd managed to track Stephen to Portsmouth as it seemed, he would hardly be looking for Stephen in the village that he now called home. He would probably have assumed that Stephen and Jessica had both died from Ricin. Unless? Unless, somehow he knew that Stephen was still alive, then he might come looking for him here.

The telephone rang loudly. It was about four in the morning and Harri's eyes shot open, and she ran with Stephen to the hallway. The phone was on an extension lead now so Stephen walked them back into the living room and sat down again on the sofa.

Sheila's tearful voice came on the telephone, which Stephen had thoughtfully put onto an open line so that Harri could join in.

"Roy is just out of surgery," Sheila answered their urgent questions. "He has lost a lot of blood and one kidney is so severely damaged that he will lose that also, but he is going to survive. He is not yet conscious, and I have been told I should not expect him to wake up for at least two days. There's no point, Harriet, in you coming down here. Your father's all wired up to all sorts of equipment and the most the doctors will allow you is to see him through a window."

"But I'll be there, Mum, I'll be there when Daddy wakes up, won't I?

"Of course, darling, but that's not going to be yet awhile. Now, what I've got to do is get me home and washed up and bring some of your dad's clothes and his pyjamas back here, so the nurses can dress him when he does come around."

"I will come to collect you, Sheila," Stephen spoke up. "Of course, I'll have to bring Harri with me, but I think a moment with her dad can be arranged and I know she needs her mother."

With everything else going on, Sheila hadn't thought of it before. "That's a point. Where is Jessica? I thought we would see her this weekend; she's not been down for about three weeks?"

"Aah well, That's another story and best told to you while we drive back here. I know enough of

Dorchester to find the hospital, so I'll see you in about an hour."

Stephen hung up before Sheila could raise an argument and asked Harri if she wanted a glass of milk. "Liquid breakfast," he said. She nodded and went to the bathroom for a toilet, splashing her face to wake up. They were in the car and on the road inside fifteen minutes.

"Where *is* Jessica?" asked Harri, strapped into the front seat as Stephen drove. It was dark outside the car, and she could hardly see over the dashboard anyway. "I've missed her weekend visits."

Stephen had always tried to be honest with her. "Jessica is also in hospital," he said. "In London. I last saw her yesterday, but her mum and dad are with her."

"Is she ill then?"

"She has been very ill," Stephen told her, "but she is going to get better," more to himself than to Harri. "And when she does, she'll look forward to seeing you and everyone else down here."

"I hope she gets to see my dad again," Harri said mournfully. It would be awful if..." She broke down with a sob.

"Hey now," said Stephen, reaching across and squeezing her hand. "Your dad's going to be all right, I'm sure. He's a toughie, isn't he. Do you remember the last time we had something like this?" Stephen was remembering Harri's abduction and Roy's heroic act of rescue.

"Yes, but *you* got hurt then," said Harri. "And now it's *my* Dad!" Out of the mouths of babes, thought Stephen.

Stephen wondered what he could say. "Your dad will be fine, Harri. It will take time, but he'll be okay eventually and then we'll all settle down to the quiet village life, just you wait and see."

"But you were right about one thing," he decided to tell her. "Your observations were bang on, even though none of us thought it could be true. It's not easy for adults to trust the judgement of a child, especially one as young as yourself. We see ourselves as the teachers, nurturers, and can't always accept a child's opinion on something. But you were right. Your teacher, Mr Cartwright, was killed. And probably by the tramp you saw, who was almost certainly the bad man that kidnapped you. We all thought he was behind bars in prison, but I've found out since that he was released last year and sent to his home in Russia. It would seem that he has returned. I just hope it isn't the same man that did this to your dad!" He left out his thoughts about the cause of Jessica's poisoning, and nearly his own.

They were almost in Dorchester town centre and Stephen saw what he thought was a sign for the hospital. A big red H confirmed it and Stephen drove up to and through the main gate and was directed to a car park for Accidents & Emergencies. Harri had the door open before Stephen had properly stopped and ran across to bury her head in her mother's skirts. Sheila was stood at the entrance to the hospital department. Stephen gave her a quick hug and they all went inside. It was just after five and the morning light was spreading into the sky.

Stephen showed his Naval ID and persuaded the nursing staff to allow Harri to see her father, They agreed but only through an observation window they said, and a young nurse took Harri to the room where Roy was recovering. Stephen and Sheila followed, Stephen with a cup of coffee quickly bought from a vending machine. Sheila didn't want anything.

"Tell me about Jessica," said Sheila as she watched her young daughter looking at her father through the window. She was sat in the corridor with Stephen, where the pair of them looked exhausted for different reasons, Stephen realising he had not slept properly since Jessica was taken ill while Sheila was just emotionally drained by the night's events.

"Jessica is in hospital in London," Stephen began, knowing that he had told this story, or almost all of it to Harri earlier. "She is recovering now, but she was poisoned in Portsmouth last Sunday with Ricin."

"Ricin!" Sheila was shocked. "But isn't that..."

"Really bad stuff, I know," Stephen interrupted her. "Yes, but Jessica saved herself by her quick action of contacting my boss, Sir Geoffrey, and he got her admitted to a specialist hospital straightaway. I am grateful to the doctors and nurses there for saving her life."

"But why would someone want to poison Jessica?"

Sheila asked. "And Ricin is not something you can just pick up from a pharmacy!"

"No. It's not. But if you know what you're doing it can be manufactured from castor beans, and you can get hold of those."

"Not easily, I wouldn't think," said Sheila. "It's not something that shops would normally carry. I never have anyway."

"No, but," Stephen knew he would have to be straight with Sheila, "in my line of work, we learn ways of acquiring what we need and where we need it."

"Your line of work?" Sheila raised an eyebrow. "But you are in the Navy?"

"The line of work I do for Sir Geoffrey, I mean. Let's just say that I sort out problems the MoD and Her Majesty's government are having around the world, and we, the kind of person I am, learn to do all sorts of things to survive when we are in the field."

"You'll remember of course, Harri's abduction and Mrs Smith's death by those Russian KGB men. Well, they were pursuing me, and I unwittingly brought them to the village. It seems that I killed one of their colleagues while away on a mission, and the man we put away for Mrs Smith's murder is still bent on revenge.

"But he's ..."

"In jail? That's what we all thought," said Stephen. "But no, I found out recently that Nikolai Volkov was returned to his own country, Russia, last August, in an exchange deal for two of our own agents. And Harri was right all along. Her teacher was killed, and almost certainly by the tramp she identified as the bad man who kidnapped her!"

"John Cartwright? The inquest verdict said a heart attack was the cause of his death."

"And it was," Stephen persisted. "But the cause of that heart attack was not his obesity, in fact he was quite a fit man given his size. It was an air embolism, a bubble of air injected into his heart that caused a cardiac arrest."

"How the ..."

"Never mind the how. A second autopsy found an injection mark in his heart and that was their conclusion. And the pathologist was asked to keep quiet about the real cause of death so as not to scare the locals, and also I suspect because she missed it the first time around."

"So, are you saying we have you to thank for all the bad stuff that's happened these past two years?" Sheila was suddenly angry. "And do you think Roy was attacked by this same man, the tramp, whoever he might be? He's not been seen by anyone in the village for over two months. I still think he was a passing traveller on his way to the coast!"

"The evidence I have accrued is stacked up against that, Sheila. As for Roy's attacker, I don't know. It's not as if Ashfield has any history of this kind of incident."

"No, I suppose not. So we have to think of the

perpetrator coming from outside the village, but why now? And why Roy!?"

"Why Jessica? Why, for that matter John Cartwright? I just don't know, but all my instincts point at Nikolai Volkov being involved in all of this."

HARRI HAD JOINED them by this time, and asked her mother if they could go home. The little girl was worried about her dad but was glad to have seen him, and now she needed her bed. The nurse she had been escorted by said it would be okay to visit again later in the day, although she should not expect her father to be awake and Harri was glad not to be pushed away. Stephen walked Sheila and Harri to his car and they drove back to Ashfield. It was nearly seven a.m. He needed sleep himself, and a Dhobi as sailors will call it, a shower. He had already decided that Church would be given a miss today, they wouldn't be expecting him anyway, and he didn't think Sheila or Harri would go either.

"I'll drive myself back to the hospital later, Stephen," said Sheila when they got back. "I'm still trying to get my head around all you've told me, and it's going to be difficult to trust you with Harri in the future when I think she might be at risk. I just want my husband home and for all this bad stuff to go away."

"I'm sorry to hear you say that, Sheila," Stephen was troubled by her words. "I haven't wanted for any of this, and I would never let anything bad happen to Harri. Or Roy for that matter. But I will have to report back to Sir Geoffrey today, and we will have to find whoever has done this. It will be like chasing shadows, but I must succeed for the sake of all of us. I too want to know what it's like to live in a quiet Dorset village with not too much excitement going on."

They parted but not on good terms. Stephen went home, deciding to dhobi first, then catch a few hours of sleep before he spoke with Sir Geoffrey or find out how Jessica was doing. He was too tired to think straight.

NIKOLAI VOLKOV WAS by this time, many miles away. He had slept uncomfortably in the small Datsun during the night by pulling off the road at a farmer's gateway but had moved on at first light. He was tired and thirsty as he drove through Milton Abbas and turned right onto The Street leading to Lake Lodge. He wasn't sure where he was going so he headed broadly south until he spotted a 7-11 store that was open at Milborne St Andrew. He bought a ready-to-eat meat pie and a large bottle of still water and sat in the shop car park having his breakfast. He wanted to keep off the main roads, but he would need petrol soon, so he had to risk the car showing up on a traffic camera. Studying the road map, he could take the A354 as far as Puddletown and then go south again on a minor road. He wanted to get somewhere where he could pinch another car; this one sounded rough as if the guts were going to fall out of it and he didn't want to draw attention to himself. He knew roughly where he was being drawn to, but it would take him a while to negotiate the unfamiliar country lanes.

STEPHEN WAS WOKEN up by the telephone at about four in the afternoon. He blearily staggered downstairs to answer it. He and Jessica had agreed not to have a phone extension put in the bedroom, that's partly why he had such a long lead on it, but there were times when it could be warranted.

Sir Geoffrey spoke first. "I've been trying to get hold of you, lad. Three times I've called!"

Stephen was initially alarmed. "Jessica?"

"No. Nothing wrong there. The hospital says she's doing well and can sit up for a while, but I expect you'll call yourself later today. No, I wanted to call and tell you we've had a sighting."

"Already," Stephen was fully awake now. "That was quick. Where?"

"Yes, well, it's a sighting and some bad stuff too. A woman called on her elderly neighbour this morning in Britannia Road, Portsmouth, because he hadn't collected her newspapers from the local shop, a regular errand apparently, and found him dead in bed in his front room. The police got called in, took forensics with them, and by the signs of it he has died of a poisoning. I haven't got the fullest of details yet, but they found a near empty bag of barley sugar sweets on the hall table."

How Sir Geoffrey found out this stuff so regularly and so quickly, Stephen had yet to learn.

"Barley sugar," said Stephen. "So you are thinking this could be the old man that Jessica met with."

"Not this man, Stephen. His lodger! His neighbour is telling the police that the old man has a lodger, but they can find no evidence of anyone else living there."

"But you said a sighting, sir? Of this lodger?"

"Britannia Road is in Fratton, Stephen, so I pulled the CCTV from the local train station and started looking backwards from yesterday and Bingo! Our man, who I'm fairly sure is Volkov, caught a train going to Cardiff, Wales, yesterday morning. The Portsmouth police have shown the pictures to the neighbour and although they are never the clearest, she is ninety per cent certain he is Mr Johnston's lodger. Mr Johnston is the name of the dead man by the way."

"And, Stephen. The lodger whom she spoke with occasionally had a foreign accent and her neighbour, Mr Johnston, 'liked men, if you know what I mean' was the way she put it to the police."

"And he might have turned up here, in Ashfield!" Stephen told Sir Geoffrey all about the attack on Roy Jasper, who was in a critical state in Dorset County Hospital in Dorchester, but who was likely to recover although he would lose a kidney that had been damaged in the attack.

Sir Geoffrey was surprised, "It's amazing that Volkov, if it is him, got there so quickly. I'm going to have to look at train routes now, to see how that's possible, but if it is, it's a real escalation of his methods. The Russians usually like more stealth, something that can't be pinned directly on them. He must be getting desperate."

"Train routes wise, I can help you there, sir," Stephen could see it in his mind's eye. "There's an hourly service from Portsmouth to Cardiff on most days, and there's plenty of stations around here. He could have changed at Salisbury and caught a West of England train to Gillingham Dorset, or Templecombe, or Sherborne. Or he could change trains at Southampton Central and ride the mainline London to Weymouth as far as Dorchester, although that's further away from the village. My guess would be Sherborne. I've had to do it myself before now and there's a regular bus service from Sherborne straight into Ashfield. If you pull the tapes from that station, say two to three hours after this man left Fratton, you may find him getting off a train there."

"But why Ashfield, Stephen? And why Roy Jasper? If Volkov is our Portsmouth man, he must assume that you and Jessica were both caught by the Ricin. He would assume you are not in the village and would have no reason to risk exposure without a specific purpose. And no disrespect to Mr Jasper, but I can't see the connection."

"Unless..." Sir Geoffrey suddenly had a thought.

"Unless," Stephen interrupted his employer, "Unless Volkov has lost face with his KGB bosses and is seeking revenge on the person he blames for that? You'll recall, when he came after me twenty months ago, on what must have been an officially sanctioned mission otherwise they wouldn't have wanted him back, it wasn't me that thwarted his attempt on my life!"

"No, it was Roy Jasper." Sir Geoffrey agreed with Stephen's reasoning. "And my guess is this is an unsanctioned mission because the KGB, as crazy as they are, would only sanction the use of knives in exceptional circumstances. Volkov, if it is him, is acting alone, and is driven by the need to rid himself not only of your shadow, Stephen, but that of anyone else who prevented him completing his mission the last time."

"And now we have to chase his shadow, Sir Geoffrey, and I'm not sure where he would go next."

"Let's try and confirm that it is Volkov we're after first. I appreciate we might need patience, but Mr Jasper may have identified his attacker so we should wait for him to regain consciousness. And Jessica can do an ID sketch for us tomorrow and we might be able to decide from that. I already have photographs from the Fratton CCTV circulating in Portsmouth and can circulate photos of Volkov if it is him we're after, to police stations nationally and especially down your way. Then we shall see what we can pick up."

Sir Geoffrey said he would get the Sherborne CCTV pictures and look at Jessica's ID sketch tomorrow. The two men agreed on what to do after that and hung up their telephones.

STEPHEN DECIDED NOT to wait. He picked up the phone and called Jane Kemp.

"Hello. Plain Jane's." Jane had her business voice on.

"Hello Jane, it's Stephen."

"Hello Stranger," said Jane. "I expected you would call. I've had Sheila on the phone to tell me about Roy and about Jessica and all that's been going on. Personally, I don't blame you for any of it, but it's a bad business all around."

"It is, yes," Stephen agreed. "And it's not going to get any better anytime soon. Look, I hate to cut you short but, is Eddie home?"

"Yes he is, but..." Jane was worried, "you're not going to get him involved are you? He's only a kid!"

"But not a child," said Stephen, "and I need to find out where the bad guy has gone. I think he's left the area, but I thought that before and he turned up right in front of me. Your Eddie knows the area outside the village like the back of his hand and I want to use his knowledge to prove that Volkov, the Russian, has left the district. Please, let me talk to him?"

"I don't want Eddie put in danger, Stephen!" said Jane, but she let Eddie take the call, nevertheless.

"Hello, Mr Lodge, it's been a long while!"

"It's been so long, Eddie, that you've forgotten to call me Stephen."

Silence...

"Have I got this right: your exams are over and you're not at school tomorrow?"

"That is correct," said Eddie, who was just starting his post-school era, "next stop is results in a few weeks' time, and then an apprenticeship."

"Any thoughts yet?" Stephen was making small talk.

"Not really. I've asked a few companies and British Rail have come up with the best offer so far, but I would have to go away to Salisbury or Bath, or maybe even Exeter for training and I'm not too keen on that."

"We can talk some more about that, but, listen, I have a problem and I think you can help me."

"What's that, Mr Lodge... Stephen?"

"Can I come by tomorrow morning, about nine, and I'll tell you both all about it?" He guessed that Jane was listening to their conversation.

There was a muffled conversation on the other end of the line and then Eddie's voice came back on."

"That will be good, Stephen. The twins should be gone by that time, so we'll get some peace and quiet. I need something to do anyway." Eddie had twin brothers, Peter and Paul, a year younger than Harri and at her school.

"Thank you, Eddie. Please, may I have a word with your mother again?"

It sounded like the phone clicked off, but that was only Eddie hanging up the extension. Jane came back on the line.

"Yes, Stephen?"

"Did Sheila say if she was sending Harri to school tomorrow?"

"No, not tomorrow, and not all week," said Jane. "In fact, I don't think Harri will go back to school this term. The kids break up in just over two weeks, heaven forbid! The Summer holidays are upon us all too soon."

"Well, I for one am glad if she doesn't go to school," said Stephen strongly. "I know it's important and all that, but the poor girl is traumatised by all that's gone on and she can do without the other kids taking a rise out of her."

"I think you need to go and make your peace with Sheila, Stephen. She's going to need your help, especially when Roy comes home, and Harri also."

"Yes, well, we've all got our hands full at the moment," Stephen spoke guardedly, "but I'll come up to your place near nine tomorrow morning and we'll talk some more then."

He hung up before Jane could say any more.

NIKOLAI VOLKOV KNEW he'd have to risk it. He hadn't seen a petrol station yet, and he knew from the black smoke trailing behind the Datsun that there was something seriously wrong with the car. He had to stick with the main road, the A35, going through

Dorchester and did eventually find a roadside service station where he could buy petrol and also food. He turned the engine off knowing that he could hotwire it again, but he didn't think that was the worst of his worries. He lifted the bonnet and a pall of dark smoke drifted off the engine block. Nikolai knew enough to recognise when a car engine needed oil and purchased a large tin of that as well. Money was becoming a challenge to him, and he would need to resort to his usual modus operandi when on a long mission: steal whenever he got the chance. After he had filled the petrol tank to halfway and poured oil into the engine block, he continued his journey. From here he would take a vaguely familiar country route to Abbotsbury, where he had once gone with Dmitri Mikhailov. He would need to find somewhere he could spend the night.

Chapter 11

In pursuit of a ghost

STEPHEN WAS UP early on Monday morning and went to see Sheila and Harri before going to Plain Jane's. Sheila's frosty reception he put down more to her tiredness than outright hostility, but Harri was pleased to see him and told Stephen they had been to the Dorset County to see her dad again.

"And we'll go again today, won't we, Mum?" she asked Sheila.

"Yes, but I am going to open the Store for the morning first," said Sheila, "and if you want to make yourself useful, young lady, you can design a colourful poster that I can put in the window telling customers I will only be open from nine until one all this week."

Harri thanked her mother for the chance to help and went off to her room to find paper and coloured pencils. She was good at drawing and was confident she could do something.

Sheila looked at Stephen. "I have to make some effort here," she told him, "but I really just want to spend all my time with Roy at the hospital."

"That's understandable, Sheila, and I'm here to support you, but I'd be no good at running your store. I can look after Harri, though, if you'll let me?"

Sheila looked at him with sadness in her eyes. "I know I spoke harshly yesterday, Stephen, but I am wary of putting Harri into danger. I know you can't be responsible for Roy's attack on Saturday, but badness is casting a shadow over our village, and it centres on you, so, until you can be certain this bad Russian man has finally been dealt with, it will affect our relationship, and our friendship."

"I am starting my search for Roy's attacker today," Stephen was hurt by Sheila's comments, but understood where they were coming from. "We are ninety per cent certain it is the Russian, but how he has been tracking me to Portsmouth, where Jessica was poisoned, and back to here is unclear."

"I will find him, Sheila, and I will deal with him more decisively this time. Unfortunately, when dealing with a foreign criminal, it's not such a straightforward affair. Politics tend to get involved and inter-country relationships must be protected. We think that Nikolai Volkov..."

"I'm not interested in politics, Stephen!" Sheila interrupted him angrily. "All I want is for you to catch my Roy's attacker, and the man who kidnapped Harri the year before last and get him out of our hair once and for all. Ashfield is used to being a quiet place to live, a centre for tourists to come and walk the Downs and explore the Vales. A place for our children to grow up safe in. We don't need international politics here!"

"Now it's time for me to get on," and Sheila busied herself getting ready to open the store. "I'll just have to telephone Roy's works and tell them he won't be in for a while."

"I could do that for you, Sheila," pleaded Stephen.

"No!" she shouted. "Just leave us to get on with things here and go and catch the bad guy!"

Stephen left the store with his tail between his legs.

"MORNING, JANE," HE said when he arrived at the former North Dorset Railway station, now home to Jane and her family.

"Hello, Stephen. Eddie's waiting on you. I'll make you a coffee and then listen in if you don't mind?"

"That's okay. I've spoken with Sheila as well this morning. That didn't go too well."

"I know she's mad with you," said Jane, "and I might be too, depending on what you've got to ask Eddie."

"Well, let's get on, shall we."

Stephen walked to the back of the tearoom and shook hands with the seventeen-year-old Eddie.

"I haven't seen you since the Christmas before last, Eddie. That's more than eighteen months ago. How's it been?"

"Good, Mr... Stephen" Eddie still couldn't get used to calling an adult by his first name. "I've finished school now, and although Dad's accepted I'm not going onto the rigs, he will want me to get something soon as."

"How did your exams go?" asked Stephen.

"I'm confident of my results, particularly in tech drawing and Math. English should be alright too. I am still keen on Engineering as a career."

"I can't talk you into the Royal then. I still think we could make an artificer out of you. And it could lead on to a commission as well. Become an officer, like me."

"And be gone for months on end," smiled Eddie. "What would Mum do then. She'd be lost without me around."

"Mum would be fine," said Jane as she brought Stephen's coffee. "You forget sometimes, my lad, it's me that takes care of you, not the other way around."

"And besides," Stephen interjected, "you'd only be based at Plymouth, or maybe Portsmouth where I've been for the last couple of months. You'd get plenty of opportunity to get home from there, about once a month I should think. You wouldn't even go to sea for the first three years, and the apprenticeship would set you up for civvy work as well whenever you come out. That's more than I've got to look forward to; I'm just a simple sailor."

"I doubt if there's anything simple about what you do, Mr Lodge," Eddie responded, "and I don't rule anything out for my future. But let's talk about the now: what is it you want me to do?"

Jane had sat down now at a nearby table, so Stephen began. "You'll know that Roy Jasper was attacked on his way home from the pub on Saturday night. He's in a pretty bad way, got stabbed in the back and he'll lose a kidney but otherwise, he'll survive."

"We believe, Sir Geoffrey and I, that the Russian we caught October before last is back in this country and was his attacker!"

"Nikolai Volkov?" said Eddie. "I thought he was sent to prison."

"He was, and then he was released in exchange for two agents of ours the Russians were holding. Volkov went back to Russia, but he has returned, we think on an unsanctioned mission, to have another pop at me."

"But what has he got against you, Stephen?" It was Jane's turn to ask a question. "Why come all this way just to find you?"

Stephen thought for a moment before he answered the question. He wanted to be open with them and realised that in fact they knew little about what he did other than being in the Royal Navy.

"Volkov and I have history," he told them. "We are in some ways the same creature. We both work for our governments, getting involved in international situations and sometimes..." he hesitated, "getting rid of the individuals involved."

He carried on quickly before his audience could ask too many questions. "Two years ago, I was sent to Saigon to assassinate a Vietnamese chemist who was experimenting with biofuels and other stuff. I failed in my mission when I decided I had been sent for commercial reasons, which is not something I want to be party to, instead of a military one which I will happily do to protect our country."

Jane and particularly Eddie were both shocked at these revelations but kept quiet and just listened.

"Anyway, I was wrong about the chemist, who was in fact developing what we call a bioweapon, and he has now been swallowed up by Chinese Intelligence. No doubt, that will come to bite us all in the bum one day. But the Russians were also after him and in saving the chemist, I killed one of their agents. Don't look so shocked! It happens all the time, more often than either you or I like, believe me."

"Volkov has some particular tie with this dead agent and has been seeking revenge ever since. His last mission was clearly with the permission of his KGB bosses but this time we think he is acting alone. So far, he has targeted me but not yet struck. Jessica, who is recovering from Ricin poisoning in a London hospital," Jane gasped, "and now Roy Jasper."

"We also believe he is responsible for the death of the teacher, John Cartwright, whom we know was killed and did not die of a simple heart attack."

Eddie didn't personally know John Cartwright even though he had been a teacher at the Church of England primary school in Ashfield for many years, but he knew the story and had followed the inquest with his mother.

"And I heard yesterday that an elderly man in Portsmouth has been killed, we think by Ricin poisoning, although we are waiting on the Path lab for confirmation. Portsmouth is where we think Jessica was poisoned also."

"And all this is down to one man, Stephen?" said Jane, now concerned not just for Eddie, but for her twin eight-year-olds also, who were at school.

"We think so, and that's where you come in, Eddie. We need to find him."

"Hey, whoa, wait a minute!" said Eddie, horrified at the thought. "I'm not going up against some veteran KGB agent who might shoot my head off!"

"And I don't want you to," said Stephen. "But you know this area better than I do – better than most I would say from your bike expeditions and such, and what I need to do is prove that Volkov is not still in the vicinity of Ashfield. I can call on the Special Branch again, I've already got two men working out of Blandford Camp, and I can trawl around myself. But you know the likely hiding places, Eddie, the places we don't."

"But he'll still be at risk," Jane was very worried now.

"It's all right, Mum," said Eddie before Stephen could reply, "he is right. I do know my way around better than Dad ever did, and particularly close to the village. I know well enough when to keep my head down, and as long as I don't have to confront this man, this Russian, directly, I should be okay."

"There's to be no confrontation," Stephen interjected. "Just report back to me. I don't even think that Volkov will hang around. We believe that he thinks I am dead, that's why he left Portsmouth behind, and where he's gone we don't know but, I just need to know he's not anywhere close by."

"I'll have to go by bicycle," said Eddie. "The scooter will be too noisy, and I haven't got much petrol in the tank anyway. Beside I'll need to go across fields and the like so it's easier to take the BMX."

"You can have all the petrol you want after we get this done, Eddie, but I agree, the bicycle will be better."

"So, let's get to it," said Eddie, and went off to find his cycle clips. He wouldn't need a coat; the day's weather forecast was warm summer sun all day.

"Look after my boy, Mr Lodge," said Jane sternly. "I don't want anything bad to happen to him." And she took his empty coffee cup back to the kitchen.

"OKAY. EDDIE," SAID Stephen as they assembled outside. "If you could cover the same ground as last time, up to Stillmoor and Tolworth Down, and I will take the road to Ashdown, Haywards Lane I think it is called. The Special Branch will be waiting for me at Farthing Corner House, Sir Geoffrey called them yesterday, and I will get them to go west toward Fifehead Church and then walk over Sturminster Common. Remember, we should be looking for someone on their feet looking like a tramp or traveller, that's the disguise that has suited

Volkov best so far."

Eddie replied, "I'll look in on Mr Walker at Fennel Farm first up. He grazes his cattle and sheep on Ashfield Hill so, he might have seen something."

They dispersed, having agreed to meet back at the tearoom by three in the afternoon. Stephen was glad that he had telephoned Jessica the evening before because he wasn't going to get much chance today. They had chatted for twenty minutes before she got hustled off the phone, probably by a nurse, and he was happy that she sounded so good. Her voice was still weak, and he could hear her breath wheezing so, still some lung problem but, comparatively, she had improved from when he last saw her, which, when he thought about it was only Saturday morning. So much was happening, and so fast that Stephen wasn't even sure what day it was.

SURE ENOUGH, WHEN Stephen got back to the cottage, SB1 and SB2 were waiting for him, and so was the Vicar and Police-Sergeant Ronald Blake. The Special Branch officers were dressed in country clothes, which they must have acquired after they were sent down to Blandford Camp. It was so unusual to see them in anything other than their smart black suits, and Stephen was amused to notice they still wore their "SB" badges pinned to their dark blue Parka's. Identity is everything, he concluded but was relieved to see them suitably attired and gave them their instructions., They left in their car to drive to Fifehead.

"What can I do for you, Vicar?" asked Stephen, "And, Sergeant Blake, what have you come to tell me?"

The policeman got in first. "I've come to tell you that you're probably wasting your time searching locally. We've had a report from Fennel Farm, from Mr Thomas Walker, of his car being stolen, probably on Saturday night, although it seems the farmer didn't notice it was gone until yesterday evening. He doesn't use it much, I'm told. I can't say for certain, but it was probably our missing suspect."

"That's good," said Stephen to the policeman's surprise. "I'm even more hopeful now that Volkov, if it is him, will have left the area. I want him as far away from this village as he can get. Today's exercise is all about trying to prove that he is *not* still close by."

"Are we not trying to catch him then?" asked Sergeant Blake. "Isn't that the job?"

"Yes, it is, Sergeant, but we are clearly dealing with a dangerous man and, if I've got my thoughts lined up like nine pins we need to strike somewhere there are not too many people about. If we can hound him into the countryside, so much the better."

"Do you think he is armed then? Should I be calling for assistance from Dorchester or even Bournemouth?"

"I don't know that he is armed but I don't put it past him to steal whatever he needs from places around. If he now has a car, he could be anywhere in the county, or even beyond, so don't get all gung-ho yet. I would like you, though, to put a policeman on the beat in Ashfield. After Saturday's incident, a little police presence would be reassuring to the locals."

"I can do that," said Sergeant Blake, "but I want you to keep me informed with everything you find, or don't as the case may be. Please remember, this is the Civvy world, not the Navy, and I am the policeman here."

"Yes, okay, Sergeant," said Stephen. "Now, Vicar, what can I do for you?"

"I am here to offer my services," James St Johns was nervous. "When I heard about poor Mr Jasper I thought how easily that could have been me, so you could say I have a vested interest."

"I'm going to cover the area up to Ashdown, so an extra pair of eyes might be useful."

"Can I suggest we go to Fiddleford and the Manor instead," said the Vicar. "The Sergeant has got to return to Ashdown anyway so he could cover that area. And I'm not just a pair of eyes, Mr Lodge, I can be a Vicar on a pastoral visit, and that will open some doors for you, particularly with the farmers."

"That's a good suggestion, Vicar. Sergeant, you okay with that?" Police-Sergeant Blake nodded.

"And, Sergeant?" Stephen added, "Did you ask Farmer Walker for the registration of his stolen car?"

"Of course I did!" the policeman bristled. "I'm not without experience, Mr Lodge. It's an easy one to remember." He took a small notebook from his top pocket and found the right page. "GUX 37V. It's a 1979 Datsun, red. Cherry by name, and cherry by colour was how Mr Walker put it, and he called his car 'Gutsy' although I am not sure why."

"Thank you," said Stephen, "I can give that description to my boss, Sir Geoffrey Cheeseman, and he can get a traffic camera search started. But we should all be on our way."

EDDIE RODE HIS bicycle directly to Fennel Farm and spoke with Mr Walker, who told him that his car had been stolen and, yes, he had reported it to the police. Eddie assumed that the police would let Stephen know but took the details of the car anyway, and noted how the farmer described his little car, which he didn't think would go far before the engine would pack up.

"She's a gutsy little thing," said Thomas Walker, "but she uses oil like she's got her own well. That's why I don't drive her much; she always needs the oil topping up for even the shortest journey!"

Eddie thanked the farmer for the information and then cycled up Ashfield Hill toward Stillmoor. He passed the Bike Park where local kids still went scrambling and saw the Pony Trek stables were already in use, so he didn't need to check there. He reached Tolworth before he turned right onto the Down, keeping an eye open for a red car possibly hidden by a tree or hedge but saw nothing. He rode across farmer's fields following public footpaths until he got to Bulbarrow Road, which led to Belchalwell

Street and back into the village. It was a warm and sunny day and Eddie had enjoyed the chance to get back on his cycle but had to agree with himself that riding the motor scooter was easier and more comfortable, just not so practical for the Downland that he'd had to cross.

ALL THE SEARCHERS returned to Plain Jane's tearoom by three o'clock. Eddie was in fact the first and glad of a sandwich and a cake from his mother's kitchen. Stephen and the Vicar arrived empty handed and without finding anything out, They had visited several farms and other homes and, as predicted, the Vicar in his dog collar had opened many of the doors, Stephen being a stranger to most of the people he met. But there had been no sign of tramps or travellers for several weeks, and certainly nothing more recent than a month. Eddie told Stephen about Mr Walker's car but, of course, Stephen already knew via the report from Police-Sergeant Blake.

"But the car won't get far," said Eddie, wanting to share some knowledge that only he had. "Mr Walker said she drinks more oil than she does water, so he wouldn't go further than fifteen miles from home and even that was stretching it."

"So Volkov won't get far enough away for my liking," Stephen responded, "I'd rather he was flying down the A35 by now. The further away the better."

The Special Branch men were last in, looking exhausted from what they regarded as a "yomp" across Sturminster Common but did have some news from the Banbury Hill Education Centre who reported they had been approached before Christmas "by a foreign gentleman" who sought food and shelter in return for helping them out with the animals, "cleaning and stabling." He worked hard too they said. And he had come back just around Eastertime to ask the same questions, but they were in full swing with their students and children by then so weren't so able to help him. Security issues, they described it as: "Every employee has to pass police checks."

"That was almost three months ago," said Stephen, "and I think we can conclude from today's exercise that Nikolai Volkov or whoever Roy Jasper's attacker is, is no longer near the village. I'll have to rely on traffic reports around the county to try and find him."

"Would he not just try to leave the country as soon as he can?" SB2 asked.

"I'm hoping not," said Stephen. "While I don't want him around the village, I am relying on him to still come after me if he thinks I am alive, but for now, all we can do is look for the car. I'll talk to Sir Geoffrey before the end of today." He was thinking it would be nice to make a flying visit to London and see Jessica but that would have to wait for now.

"Vicar, have you been to see Sheila Jasper at all, and assuming you have, how was she? I am not in her good book just now."

"I saw her this morning before I came to your

cottage, Mr Lodge" replied the Reverend. "She seemed okay; more concerned about Roy than anything. The hospital have told her that her husband is not responding well to treatment. They are worried about internal bleeding and might have to operate again to see if they've missed something first time around. It looks like he'll stay under until at least Friday, they are saying."

"Sir Geoffrey and I were relying on Roy to identify his attacker, but that will have to wait. My Jessica is doing an ID sketch today of the man she met at Southsea Common so we might get something from that." The Vicar looked at Stephen with curiosity. "For those who don't already know, Jessica was poisoned just over a week ago with Ricin, I should have been too, but I never ate one of the sweets containing the poison. It's a bit of a story and I'll tell it another time but I'm happy to report that Jessica is recovering well in a London hospital."

"Sadly, an elderly man in Portsmouth has also been poisoned with Ricin and he has since died. Sir Geoffrey Cheeseman is circulating Nikolai Volkov's photograph to all the Portsmouth and nearby police stations, but I don't think we'll find him there. We are ninety per cent sure that he was identified on CCTV catching a Cardiff train from Fratton last Saturday. That's why I think he has returned to Ashfield and is responsible for Roy Jasper's stabbing attack and that's why we're all here today."

"But isn't that all the more reason why he'd make

a run for it and try to escape from the country?" asked SB1.

"I don't think he has the resources," said Stephen in reply. "We think this is an unsanctioned mission and he doesn't have the backing of his employers. I doubt that he could even seek sanctuary at the Russian embassy in London. The KGB are notorious for turning their back on agents they've fallen out with. Usually they turn up dead by unexplained means. No, I might be overthinking it, but I think Volkov is obsessed with ridding himself of me, and now we are pursuing the ghost that haunts me all over the county. It's a real cat and mouse game, this one."

"But who is who," said the Vicar, "and surely we'll need him to come after you again, maybe even to the village, if he cannot be found beforehand."

"You are probably right, James," it was the first time Stephen had called him by his first name in public company, "but let's see what we can turn up in the search for his car. Then, maybe, I can target him more directly."

Their meeting broke up soon after. SB1 and SB2 were instructed to search the north of the county following the line of the A30 as far as Crewkerne to the west and Eddie agreed to watch out for the Ashfield and Ashdown areas. Stephen would go south and start looking along the Jurassic coastline as it was the only area he knew well.

"THERE'S BEEN A setback in Roy Jasper's condition,"

Stephen was telling Sir Geoffrey on the telephone. He had only just got home, and was hoping for news from Sheila, but she and Harri were out, probably at the hospital so he went with the news given him by the Vicar. "It seems that he might still have internal bleeding so, a second operation is planned. It could be that we don't get to talk to him until the end of the week."

"Then it's just as well that Jessica was able to work with the ID-sketcher this morning." Said Sir Geoffrey. "I could be wrong, but I would say it's a fair match for Volkov and the Fratton Station man on CCTV. Can you make it up here tomorrow morning and tell me what you think?"

"I'd be delighted to," the idea cheered Stephen up. He would get to see Jessica as well as have a day in the city, so it was a win-win for him.

"Make it by ten. I know that's an early start for you, but I know also you'll want to see Jessica."

Stephen gave Sir Geoffrey the detail and registration of the car that Volkov might be driving, and Sir Geoffrey agreed to start a search using traffic cameras before hanging up on the phone. Before Stephen could boil a kettle for tea, the phone rang again and he picked it up thinking there had been a change of plan, but it was the builder for the garage.

"Mr... Lodge?" the man was clearly reading from a note. "My name is Tony Woods of Extraordinary Woods. I'm the man you've hired to come and build your garage extension."

"Oh, yes. Mr Woods," said Stephen. "It's good to talk with you at last. My partner, Jessica, has dealt with everything until now. When was it you planned to start work?"

"That's why I've phoned," said Tony Woods. "I wasn't due until next week, but I've finished my current project early so I can start on yours on Wednesday, if that's convenient?"

"I have to tell you that it's not the best of weeks," started Stephen, "But, do you need me around?"

"No," said Tony, "Well, only to start with. It's just a question of setting up and I might need access to your toilet if that can be arranged. The sooner I start the earlier I finish, and I reckon if I get on with it this week while the weather's good, I could be finished before the end of August."

"I expect we can come to some arrangement," said Stephen, "What time do you want to start?

"I always like to start by eight and work through 'til five, weather permitting. It's a fairly straightforward job. The biggest complication is buttressing one side of the roof into the cottage wall but there'll be two of us on the job anyway, so we can just get on with it."

He continued. "I hope your partner told you we'd need half the payment up front. Materials are ordered and will be delivered in time, but I have had to pay for those already."

"I must admit I had forgotten that," Stephen admitted. "but that's okay. I am in town tomorrow and can get the cash from my bank. It was cash wasn't it?"

"Yes, please. Cash is always best. Could I ask for £1700 now and the balance of £1500 on completion, please?"

"£3200, the total," confirmed Stephen, "and that's including VAT?"

"Yes, that's right. So I'll see you at eight on Wednesday then?"

"That's fine, Mr Woods, I'll meet you here." Stephen hung up.

STEPHEN PLANNED TO go up to the Greene Dragon for a meal that evening but thought he should ring Jessica first. He got through to the hospital reception and was told she had been moved to a four-bed ward because they need the side ward for more intensive cases.

"That sounds like she's making progress," said Stephen, "so that's the good news. But I thought Jessica was in a private ward, paid for by the government?"

"Yes, she was," came the reply, "but she has agreed to move out of the single-bed ward so that we can use it for a more needy case. Your girlfriend is no longer in intensive care, Mr Lodge. You should be happy."

"I am," said Stephen. "I'm just surprised, that's all. But I will be up tomorrow so I can see for myself. If it's inconvenient to talk to her now, can I ask you to give Jessica the message that I will be in to see her before twelve o'clock."

"I'm sure she'll be very pleased to see you," he was reassured. "We are just in the throes of moving her stuff around now so, we'll see you tomorrow." The line hung up. Stephen got his coat and went up to the pub.

IT WAS ONLY normal pub grub, but Stephen was told the meat pie and chips was good for today, so he went with the recommendation, and he wasn't disappointed. Tiny Tim came across with two pints of Mendip Twister beer and sat himself down.

"You look as if you could do with a stronger brew, Stephen," he said. "So I thought I would join you. What have you done with our Jessica?"

Stephen chuckled. "My Jessica is in a London hospital but getting better every day. I have yet to see your Jessica." The friendly rivalry continued but there was only going to be one winner.

"Bad business about Roy." Tim put a serious look on. "Do you really think it was our Russian friend?"

Word was getting around, thought Stephen. "Yes, I do. But I rely on the likes of yourself to play this down, and settle any worries there are in the community. After all, Tim, I know you're on the Parish Council and that's the quasi-government in Ashfield. So it's your job to see that village life goes as normally as possible."

"Easier said than done," said Tim, "but I'll work on it. Now, is it right what's happened to Jessica?"

Stephen wondered who had been talking already, but he didn't ask. "Yes. So far, we think Nikolai Volkov is responsible for two deaths and two attempted murders. I can tell you that John Cartwright was murdered, and so was an old man, another homosexual in Portsmouth. And all of this is my fault! I have to accept that responsibility."

"Bullshit!" Tiny Tim was explicit. "What you did was your job. If it weren't for you we'd have lost Harri Jasper two years ago, and I already knew about John Cartwright. And not wanting to be unkind, John and probably the other one also, brought it upon themselves. Jessica is innocent in this, of course, and Roy Jasper as well, but just because this fanatic is after you doesn't mean you're to blame."

"Roy's been talking to you as well as the Reverend." Stephen looked straight at Tiny Tim. "So, how much do you know?"

"I know what you do working with your London boss," replied Tim. "But there's always risk in that line of work. Sometimes you fail, but if you come home, you count that as a win, and you leave the actuals on the field of play."

"Look, I did Malaysia in the early sixties, and I volunteered to go back into uniform for the Falklands in '82. War ain't nice, and if I had to accept the vengeance of all those families that I've taken fathers and brothers from, you would have to stand me up against a wall to face multiple firing squads. The nightmares are bad enough, without blaming yourself for what's happened to the others."

"What you need to do is catch this bastard and make sure he can't come back!"

"That won't be easy," said Stephen as he supped his beer, grateful for a fellow serviceman to share time with. "It's a big country and I don't know where to begin."

"He won't have gone far," said Tim. "Not if he thinks you're still alive."

"But he probably doesn't. He thinks by now that Jessica and I have died because of his clever bit of Ricin poisoning."

"Look me in the eye, Stephen. Listen to what I'm saying. He won't have gone far *if he thinks you are still alive*! It's a cat and mouse game. Perhaps it's time you became the cheese in the trap?"

Stephen knew what Tim was saying, but he did not want to entice Volkov back into the quietness of Ashfield.

"So, you'll find somewhere else to do it," said Tim, "and when you do I'll throw the bar open, and we'll have a celebration. Mind you, it could be the only time I'll see the pub full!" He laughed.

Chapter 12

Mrs Moira Russell

NIKOLAI VOLKOV HAD a stroke of good fortune, the first in a long while. On his way to Abbotsbury, he had pulled into the Hardy Memorial Monument where he remembered going to with Dmitri when they were following Stephen Lodge to West Bay. It was late afternoon on Sunday, and he contemplated staying here overnight, again sleeping in the car, but the real reason he had pulled over was because black smoke was once more pouring from the car exhaust. The engine would need more oil; it was a good job he had bought a large tin.

While he had the bonnet of the Datsun Cherry up and he was leaning over the hot engine looking to see if the oil was leaking from somewhere, a woman's voice hailed him.

"Got a problem there?"

Volkov turned and saw a stout woman in country tweeds, wearing breeks and sturdy boots. She looked in her early sixties, about ten years older than Nikolai, not tall, and he imagined she was out walking the dog when, sure enough, a black Highland Terrier showed up, giving Nikolai one defensive bark but otherwise keeping quiet. He looked around but could not see a car, so he guessed that she was a local.

"I'm having trouble with the oil," said Nikolai, "but I haven't got the tools to find out where the problem is, and so I just have to keep topping her up."

"And, judging by the black smoke when you came driving in, that's really bad. Have you come far today, Mr...?" The woman held out her hand to shake his.

"Petrovich. Pyotr Petrovich," said Nikolai, playing safe he thought. No one is going to be looking for Pyotr. "From the East. But I can't shake your hand, miss, mine are too dirty." And he held up his oily hands.

"Moira Russell," the woman introduced herself. "And it's Mrs. although I've been a widow for the last ten years. Look, I only live just down the road. If you think the car will make it, why don't we drive there, and you can look for tools in my husband's garage. I don't drive so they're no bloody good to me."

"But I'm a stranger, Mrs Russell," warned Nikolai. "Why would you help a stranger in this way?"

"Moira," said Moira. "We could call it a Samaritan moment. You're a visitor to the area, and from overseas by the sound of it. Russia, is it?"

Nikolai felt compelled to nod.

"So you need help. And I am a stranger to you also. But I am an old woman who's not particularly worried what people think of me, and quite capable of helping a fellow human when the need arises. I'm not scared of anything, Mr Petrovich. I've learned in these last ten years of widowhood to take care of myself. And besides, you have a broken-down car. I have a garage with bits and pieces of tools in. And I have my trusty companion, James here, to protect me." And she bent down to scoop up the little terrier and gave him a hug. In return, James gave an excited woof and licked her face.

What have I got to lose, thought Nikolai, and I could certainly do with some help.

"Thank you, Mrs Russell. Moira. I am incredibly grateful to you. If you can show me the way, please." He put the bonnet down and they got into the car. Volkov had wired the ignition up so that it stayed on so starting the engine was not a problem, although it sounded rough.

"That sounds more like my neighbour's tractor than a small car," observed Mrs Russell. "But I'm sure we'll soon have her fixed up." They only had to drive half a mile toward Abbotsbury before turning left onto a long earthen drive up to a substantial looking bungalow with an open garage standing to one side.

"Drive straight into the garage, Mr Petrovich," instructed Moira. "It's never shut. In fact, I'm not sure that the door even works now."

Nikolai did as he was told. He looked around the spacious garage and could see all sorts of paraphernalia on the shelves, not completely disorganised but not tidy either.

"My husband was related to the Bride Valley Russell's; they're an old dynasty that goes back centuries," Moira told him, "We used to own land around here, but I couldn't look after it by myself, so I sold it to the neighbouring farm with the proviso that I carried on living in the house my husband built. It's a good arrangement for me. The driveway stays clear, and the farmer has to grade it now and then to get his own vehicles onto the fields. And it's far enough off the road from Martinstown to keep it quiet but not so far that I can't walk down to the bus stop you'd have seen just when we were turning in. And James and I can go for a walk when we feel up to it up to the Monument, which is really only half a mile away cross-country. There's a lot of trails, and you have to admit, the views from Black Down are superb."

"Well, I must get on with this car, Moira," said Nikolai, who had some experience with engines. Stripping his outer coat off, he was conscious of the blood stains on it and thankful the coat was dark and grubby from weeks of wear. "Time is getting on and I am thankful for your hospitality, but I will be out of your hair just as soon as I can be."

Moira gave him a look but said she would make some tea, going into the house.

"Help yourself to whatever you need," she said, waving a hand at the shelves and tools. "I rummage around in here sometimes so don't expect the place to be tidy or organised."

Nikolai found the switch for the garage light and pushed open the bonnet on the Datsun. He also found a carjack, realising this garage probably had every tool he needed in it. He searched around the engine block for leaks, noting the intake manifold was black in places, but that was superficial. He jacked the car up and found some wooden blocks he could place under the wheels. Lying down he could see the problem straightaway; the oil filter had not been secured properly and the edges of the gasket were black and shiny with fresh oil. Nikolai thought he could fix it so long as the gasket was still in one piece.

"Tea, Mr Petrovich?" said the voice of Moira Russell. Nikolai slithered out from under the car to stare up into the face of the person in question, and then hoisted himself up to accept the mug of tea she offered.

"I assumed you'd want sugar as well, so I've brought that too," a bowl and spoon being held by the other hand.

"Thank you," said Nikolai, grateful for the hot liquid into which he spooned three measures of sugar to make it sweet. "And please, call me Pyotr."

"Can you fix it, Pyotr? The car I mean?"

"Yes, but it's going to take an hour or two. Still, the daylight is good for the moment and the electric light in here is helpful. The trickiest part of this is salvaging enough oil from the sump to be able to use it again and even that depends on how good the old oil is."

"If it's ordinary oil you need, there's a whole drum of the stuff under that work bench," Moira waved a hand at one corner of the garage. "My husband looked after all his own vehicles but the stuff's no use to me."

"But you are going to get filthy, Pyotr, and I don't have an overall that I can lend you. And it will be probably too late for you to get back on the road, so why not stop for the night. No hanky-panky: I have a second bedroom doing nothing but collecting dust, and you're very welcome to stay. And, if you don't mind my saying so, you look as if you could do with a good night's sleep."

Nikolai couldn't believe his luck at meeting this kind English woman but didn't want to appear too eager.

"You are truly kind, Moira, but I do not want to cause you any problems. It's true, I have been on the road for days, travelling down from the North of your country and I have been sleeping in the car when I can to keep my costs down."

"But you don't know anything about me" he warned, "and I certainly do not deserve such kind treatment. Why would you do this?"

"Let's just say I like a bit of excitement," Moira responded, "and it's been quite a while. I'll be glad of the company and perhaps you can tell me a little about your travels in England. For all that I love the company of my dog, James, it is nice to have another human to talk with occasionally."

And with that, Moira walked back to the house to see what she could knock up for dinner. She looked forward to an evening of interesting conversation. She might even put a skirt on, she thought.

Nikolai got to work on the car. He was used to turning his hand to many things, acknowledging that he had learned ways to keep him going between missions and even on missions as difficulties cropped up. And one of those difficulties was now: he was not used to being treated so kindly and wondered what stories he could concoct to entertain his host for the evening. But he recognised good luck when he came upon it and thought he should make the most of his opportunity.

He placed a bowl under the engine sump and carefully removed the oil filter. It was badly clogged up, so he knew he was going to have to drain the sump of old oil. He found the drum that Moira had referred to and was relieved when he realised it still had almost five gallons still in it. He also found some lighter oil that he thought would help him clean the filter and the sump well. He was riding his luck now and the filter gasket was still in one piece and reusable with a bit of manipulation.

When he had finished all that he needed to do and checked the exhaust manifold and cleaned up the engine block, he was pleased with his achievements.

It had taken the best part of two hours, but he was sure the car would run much better now. He was tired and grateful for the offer from Mrs Russell of a good night's sleep, but he would need to be on his way early in the morning. Nikolai thought that the more he loitered here, the more that Moira would find out about him, and that put her at risk of needing to be silenced.

"Why don't you have a bath before dinner," she said to him when he went across to the bungalow. "Your clothes are filthy; there's a whole wardrobe of my husband's clothes in your bedroom and I'm sure you'll find something that fits."

"Thank you, Moira," Nikolai replied. "If you are sure. I'm not sure what I'll do with this shirt and trousers, but I do have another set in my backpack, although they do need washing."

"That's not a problem either. I can put them through the washing machine for you."

"Now you are being too kind, Moira," insisted Nikolai, thinking of Roy Jasper's blood on his clothes. "But I'll do that. I am well used to looking after my own things back home since my parents died."

"All right," said Moira. "Was that recent? Your parents, I mean."

"No, they've been gone five years now. But I'll clean up and if we can have some dinner, I'll tell you what I've been up to since then."

Nikolai was shown to his room and where everything was and quickly acquired some clothes that would fit him well enough, a pair of cords and a blue denim shirt. He ran a bath and was glad of a soak and almost dozed off in the warm soapy water. He showered his hair and washed several days of travel out of himself and then went to dinner with Mrs Moira Russell. He noticed she had changed and was wearing a skirt and he hoped, given her advanced years she wasn't getting any notions of romance. That would add complications to his time here.

They ate a light meal of a Chicken Caesar Salad, and the Russian was grateful to have real food in his belly. When they finished he helped Moira with the washing up before she produced a bottle of white wine and they repaired to the living room. Under questioning, Nikolai told her how difficult it was to get out of communist-controlled Russia but since his parents died within months of each other over five years ago, he had wanted to explore the world. So far, England was the only country he had managed to visit.

"Where is home, Pyotr," asked Moira.

Nikolai replied, "In Kovalevo, a small town about fifty miles east of the centre of Leningrad, although we always knew it as St Petersburg. My father was a metal worker in the town, but he liked to fish in the Reka Zin'kovka, the river that runs through the village, most of all."

"And how did you get to England eventually?" Moira was curious about her Russian visitor.

"It actually wasn't too difficult in the end. My

father died last, and we did not have a home of our own, so I had to move out of the village. I went to the city and volunteered as a crewman on a container ship to Holland. From there, I took a ferry from Rotterdam to Hull."

"Are you telling me you are an illegal immigrant, Pyotr?"

"No, no. Not really. I persuaded the purser on the container ship, with just a little bit of a bribe, to grant me a twelve-month visitor's visa." Nikolai chuckled at his easy ingenuity but needed to keep up the lies. "And I can stay until the end of August. but I must return to my country by then."

"How long have you been over here then," Moira was intrigued, "and what have you been doing with yourself?"

"I've been here since December. I set myself the task of travelling through as much of the country as I can, but your country is a lot more expensive than mine and I have had to work my way also, to stay afloat as you might say. I bought my old car in Hull when I landed, and she has been good with me but has had this oil problem only since we came south of Oxford. And I had hoped to travel the coastline to your Plymouth in Cornwall."

"Devon, Pyotr. Plymouth is in Devon," corrected Moira. "But that's neither here nor there. What happens after that?"

"I get passage as a crewman back to Holland or Denmark, and then travel back into my country via one of our Baltic republics."

"You make it sound so simple. You must have been planning this a long time."

"I am not alone in wanting to explore the world outside of the USSR or my country, Russia, Moira. Young men dream all the time, but the opportunities do not present themselves easily with our government restrictions. It has taken me all these years to look at maps and dream of freedom to explore and, even then, I could not do it while my parents were still living. They would be at risk of penalties if it were noticed that I was missing."

Moira had poured herself a second glass of wine and sidled a little closer on the sofa they were sharing. Nikolai declined the wine, which he found too sweet.

"But won't you get into trouble anyway, when you do return, Pyotr? To your country?"

"By then, I will have done what I came to do," Nikolai responded, not shying away from this curious Englishwoman. "I will have completed my journey and I will take whatever fate befalls me."

"Well, I have a few jobs you could do for me," Moira smiled at him. "So, why don't you stay a few days here and I'll give you a list in return for board and lodgings. And then we can get your coat cleaned up; it looks like a tramp's coat, and I notice it's got some blood on it."

"Oh, that!" Nikolai was alarmed but thought quickly. "I came across a sheep while I was travelling around, and it had got caught up in some barbed wire at the edge of the road. It was a mess and covered in blooded scratches, and I managed to untangle it and get it back into a field."

"Aah, you see," said Moira. "That's why you were brought to my attention today. One good turn deserved another!"

After that, they both cleared up and went to their separate bedrooms. Nikolai counted his Russian chickens again and thought it wouldn't do any harm at all to spend a few days here helping Mrs Russell with some jobs. He stripped off and slipped into the comfortably warm bed naked as he preferred. He was just drifting off to sleep when Mrs Russell came quietly into his room in her nightie and slipped into the bed next to him.

"This is the first of those jobs I talked about, Pyotr. Even a woman of my years can have needs, and it's been a long time since I slept with a man in my bed."

Nikolai and Moira made love, and they both went to sleep smiling.

VOLKOV WOKE ON Monday with a contented smile still on his face. Moira had already left his bed and might have gone back to her own room, but he could hear movement he thought from the kitchen area. He got up and showered and put some clothes on, the same as he had yesterday, and walked into the kitchen where he could smell good coffee.

"Nothing quite like it to start the day," said Moira,

who had her happy head on this morning. "The Americans at least got something right."

"How long do you think you'll be able to stay?" she asked Nikolai. "I can give you a short list or a much longer one."

"I shall want to leave by Friday morning," replied Nikolai, "but after last night, I can guess what might be at the top of your list." He laughed.

"Let's not get too carried away, Pyotr," Moira's words let him down gently. "I'll certainly come back for more, but you've got places to go, and I'll need my quiet life back soon enough. Friday morning will be fine for me."

Nikolai was relieved: no clingy lover, unlike the unfortunate John Cartwright.

"I'll do eggs and bacon for breakfast, while you have a look at that list. First up this morning is to get my washing line back up. If only so we can dry your clothes out on what looks like another sunny day."

Nikolai enjoyed a second cup of coffee and his eggs and bacon and then took the jobs list outside to see what was to do. The washing line post had blown down in a strong wind, Moira said, and probably with too much washing on the line, so Nikolai found a step ladder, and a hammer and nails, and did some preparatory work on the ground before hammering the eight-foot post back into the hole he had made. He took a couple of lengths from an old picket fence and drove them into the ground as well, nailing them to the post to form a supportive "V" shape. He wasn't the quickest of workers, but he had all day and wanted to spin out his week with Mrs Russell because it would keep him off the road and out of sight. He wandered across the driveway to a clump of trees and found a long slim branch with a fork at one end. He only needed about ten feet, so he crafted a pole to use as a prop for the washing line. Mrs Russell approved when he explained it would lift her washing higher, but it would also add support against the wind whichever way it blew. Even his hooded coat got cleaned.

The Russian enjoyed his first day of normality in a long time. It reminded him of home helping his mother and father with their daily tasks between his missions abroad. Of course, they wouldn't approve of his relationship with Pyotr, who only lived a couple of streets away, but it was a small village and tongues would wag. His parents probably knew but said nothing and he had a good relationship with them.

And for now at least, he was with Moira and the days passed by quickly, but the nights lasted forever. He enjoyed her company and her body, past its best for sure but so was he. It was soon Thursday evening, and he thought of all the jobs he had helped her with -- cleaning out gutters and drains, tidying and organising the garage just so, she said with a laugh, she could take another ten years making it untidy again. Mowing the lawn and cutting back the shrubs, lighting a bonfire every night with the detritus of each day's efforts. He even walked out with Moira and James on Wednesday when they went for their daily constitutional to the Hardy Monument, and she pointed to the different places of interest they could see along the coastline. It was an enjoyable time for both of them.

As they lay in bed together on Thursday night, they both knew their time had run its course.

"Perhaps you'll come back this way again, Pyotr," she said quietly as she snuggled into his side.

"Don't wait too long for me," he responded. "I doubt I'll be allowed to, assuming anyway I can get back into my country. The Berlin Wall may only separate East and West Germany, but the borders of the USSR are closely guarded all the way north through the Baltic and across Finland. I have enjoyed this week with you, Moira, and I thank you for everything you've allowed me to do. I can't stay but I will not forget my little English rose."

They made love for the last time, and it was Nikolai's turn to rise with the dawn and be on his way.

Chapter 13

The Bride Valley

THE WEEK IN Ashfield had gone much slower. Stephen drove up to London on Tuesday and met with Sir Geoffrey. He agreed that Jessica's ID sketch looked enough like Volkov's convict photograph to be fairly certain it was the same man, and he saw the Fratton CCTV pictures as well. Sir Geoffrey was still waiting on the Sherborne tapes but both men accepted the likelihood of what they would find on those. The traffic camera search had been instigated but Sir Geoffrey was cautious about what areas they could cover. Stephen suggested the A30 to the north of Ashfield and the A35 to the south and asked if any of the minor roads had CCTV as well.

"Not much," said Sir Geoffrey. "Most of the towns and larger villages will have something but I'd have to recruit a bigger team to view all of those. Perhaps it's time we involved the police forces, particularly Dorset and Hampshire to keep a look out for this ... red Datsun Cherry?"

"You'll need to make them aware not to approach the driver unnecessarily," said Stephen. "And it might be as well to warn them of the possible international repercussions. After all, we're dealing with the Russians."

AFTER STEPHEN LEFT the office, he went to his London bank and withdrew the cash for Mr Woods the builder. He was grateful to his parents for leaving him such a large bequest in their will, most of it from the the sale of their Gillingham home, his father having paid the mortgage off while he was still working. Being an only child, apart from small charitable bequests, he inherited the entire estate. Financially, Stephen Lodge knew he was much better off than many Naval officers could ever hope to be.

He bought flowers from a street-seller near the hospital and was overjoyed to see Jessica sat up in bed with a big beaming smile when he arrived. Although she was now in a small four-bed ward there were no other patients so they could talk openly.

"Mr Woods is starting work on the garage tomorrow," Stephen told her after a lingering and long desired kiss. "He telephoned yesterday to ask if he could start the job early and said he should be finished before the end of August."

"That's great," Jessica responded, "but how is Roy? Sheila and Harri must be really worried."

"Roy will be okay, but it's going to take a while. He's had a bit of a setback and the doctors may have to operate again, but we'll know soon enough. Sheila is mad at me for bringing Volkov back to their village, and it will take me a long while to get back into her good books. I don't think that can happen until you return home."

"And that will be a while as well," said Jessica. "The doctors here say that I have too much fluid in my lungs to think about discharging me, so I have to wait."

"Are they saying you're still suffering from the Ricin? I thought they'd got rid of all that, and they've put you into this larger ward because you don't need specialist treatment."

"I'm not in need of intensive care," said Jessica, "and I volunteered to move out of the private ward so they could use it for their next patient." She squeezed Stephen's hand. "I might always have a lung problem, they tell me. I'll probably notice it most if I go for a run or visit the gym so you might have to put up with a less than fit me."

"I'm ... really ... sorry," he stammered, wanting to give his girlfriend a hug.

"Don't be silly," she said, "It's happened, and I shall have to more cautious now who I accept sweets from." Jessica laughed. "Mum and Dad will come in and see me every day, they've really settled into my flat, and I will be out of here just as soon as I can be. You should go and catch the bad guy and get him out of our hair!"

"Now you're sounding like Tiny Tim and Sheila," Stephen told her, smiling. "Sir Geoffrey says I should make more of a commitment to you, but I don't know what the Royal have planned for me, and I worry about being away too long and too often."

"Perhaps you should," Jessica reached forward and kissed him. "Take a risk, you've got a fifty-fifty chance, and I'm a big girl and can choose for myself."

They kissed again before Stephen returned to find his car and drive home.

TONY WOODS CAME before eight on the Wednesday morning to start building the garage extension. Stephen moved his VIVA SL out onto the road and showed Tony the way into the utility room and the downstairs toilet and gave him a spare key for the back door.

"But help yourself to tea or coffee in the kitchen should you need it. Just leave the room tidy when you're finished for the day and do lock the back door if I am not here. I'm sure we can trust each other, Mr Woods. I may not be here much. I've got a few places around the county I need to visit. So I'll just let you get on and enjoy the good weather we are having."

ON THURSDAY, STEPHEN met at the Vicarage with James St Johns, Eddie, SB1, and SB2, to share any sightings there had been but, of course, there had been none. Sir Geoffrey had not reported any traffic sightings either, so it seemed that Volkov had either gone to ground somewhere or perhaps had fled the country after all.

"I'm surprised we haven't found the Datsun," said Eddie. "From what Mr Walker was saying, it just couldn't have gone far."

"Nothing yet, anyway," said Stephen. "But perhaps the Specials could take a drive down through the country roads to Dorchester and look out for dumped cars." SB1 and SB2 agreed that they could. "In the meantime, I think we should all go the Greene Dragon for lunch. Tim tells me he's not getting enough customers, despite it being the high season for tourists. You too, Vicar, my treat, and we'll carry on our chat down there."

STEPHEN TOOK THE call on Friday afternoon.

"We've had a sighting," said Sir Geoffrey, "in Abbotsbury earlier today. A red Datsun Cherry heading west. The registration is a bit blurry but I'm confident it's the right car."

"Abbotsbury? If you are right, he's taken a long time getting there. It's only an hour or so from here."

"Perhaps he has been holed up somewhere," Sir Geoffrey continued. "You would best get down there and see if you can pick up his trail. Visit the Swannery. Take a photograph with you. Ask around. I'll pull CCTV from the roads out of Abbotsbury, there aren't many, and will await a call from you later. My usual number. I've taken the liberty of booking you into the Three Horseshoes at Burton Bradstock, I don't think you'll get much further than that tonight. And Stephen, you'd best carry your tools. We know how dangerous Volkov can be, so let's not go taking chances!"

Stephen knew what he meant and retrieved his Walther PPK and ammunition from its hidden compartment beneath the floorboards of the back bedroom. The gun was immediately usable; he cleaned it every few days when he was at home alone. What no one else knew, not even Sir Geoffrey, was that Stephen had purchased a long-range Winchester rifle from a private dealer over a year ago and kept that and ammunition hidden in a secret compartment under the back seat of his car. He hadn't even looked at it himself since returning from Scotland but assumed it would be in working order because he kept it oiled and wrapped. He thought the Winchester was going to come in handy if he could get a sight on the Russian.

Stephen packed an overnight bag and took the fastest route he knew to Abbotsbury, passing the Hardy Monument where he had unwittingly seen the blue van that Volkov used the last time they met. He showed the photograph at the Swannery reception area, but the staff were certain they had not seen anyone fitting that description. He drove back through the village and asked at the Ilchester Arms without luck before walking along to St Nicholas Church.

Abbotsbury was a delightful village on the eastern lip of the Bride Valley, showing its age through the attractive terraced cottages built with Portland stone. The Swannery, where you could stroll amongst hundreds of Mute Swans was considered the main attraction but, if you walked there through the fields you could visit St Catherine's Chapel and look out across the English Channel beyond Chesil Beach. It was a wonderful place to be for almost the whole year, only getting bleak in the occasional bad winter. Today, it would be a gorgeous stroll in the sunshine, but Stephen did not have the time for that now.

The Bride Valley was named after the six-and-a-half-mile long River Bride that runs through it from Littlebredy in the east until the river meets the sea at Burton Freshwater, not far from West Bay, marking the end of Chesil Beach. The river name is of Celtic origin and may come from the Old Welsh, Brydi. It is an area of hard-working farms, mostly cattle and sheep, and the locals still eat their own cheeses, milk, and other dairy products.

Stephen knew that Littlebredy was in its way the source of the whole Valley; the river Bride having risen as a spring under the lake close to but west of the village. With a population of less than one hundred and twenty, junior children attended the Thorners School at Litton Cheney, while all secondary pupils in the east of the valley above the age of eleven were sent to Dorchester for schooling. To the North of the village is the Valley of Stones from which the material for many of Dorset's memorials, including the Nine Stones circle in a wooded glade just north of the A35, are sourced.

Litton Cheney was the biggest of the little villages in the Bride Valley with a population of almost four hundred, and the church of St Mary's oversees the whole of the eastern end to the valley. The village location dates back to the Iron Age and has a number of prehistoric sites surrounding it. The present day Thorners School is built on the site of a much older one, income coming from London property owned by Sir Robert Thorner of Baddesley, Southampton, in 1690, for the purpose of creating and maintaining a free school in the parish.

STEPHEN DROVE WEST on the long Abbotsbury Hill to Swyre and thought he would have time to turn right to Puncknowle, pronounced Punnoll, just in case Volkov had parked up for the night. Stephen was grateful for the time the previous year when he and Jessica had explored before he went to Scotland, so he knew the area reasonably well. He called into the Crown Inn and showed the photograph to the landlord and one or two locals but without success. One of the locals, though, thought that he had seen a red Datsun Cherry as described by Stephen earlier in the day on the main road to Swyre, but that might have just been for the pint of beer that was on offer for information.

STEPHEN RETURNED TO Swyre and continued westwards on the B3157, passing Beacon Knap and Bexington village before reaching the Three Horseshoes in Mill Street, at Burton Bradstock. It was about seven p.m. and Stephen did not expect to go on much further this night, so he ordered a pint of Huntsman Ale. Here he had more success, the barman and a local both identifying Nikolai Volkov from the photograph as passing through the village only a few hours before.

"He was in his car asking directions for West Bay," said one of them, "which is, as you might know, just a mile or two along the coast road. He didn't seem in any hurry though. What's he done?"

"Nothing really," replied Stephen. "He absconded from a rest home in the New Forest and stole a carer's car. I'm just trying to retrieve him and hopefully the car before he gets hurt. He's no threat to anyone other than himself so long as he takes his medication."

"But I have a booking for a room here tonight made by my employer. My name is Stephen Lodge."

"Aah, common mistake, We don't do B&B anymore; that will be the Anchor just up the road. The Horseshoes is the better pub, and we do great food, but the Inn stole our guest trade. Your boss must have got the wrong place. Good luck with that, it can be quite busy in the Inn; I hope he booked ahead."

Stephen finished his beer and drove the hundred and fifty yards to the Anchor Inn, where, fortunately, Sir Geoffrey's secretary, Hazel Eaves had arranged for a room.

NIKOLAI VOLKOV MEANWHILE had continued westwards, reaching West Bay, and had tucked his car into a grassy corner of the East Beach car park, paying for 24 hours with money he had stolen from Moira's house, "may she please be forgiving." He knew it would have to be a night in the car, but he could afford to get some food from the SPAR Convenience Store at the far end of the Station Yard car park. He hoped to stay local. There was a public toilet that was open until late so he could make use of it when necessary. A few tourists walked the beach in the evening sun, waiting for it to set over the headland to the west, but they were of no interest to him. As long as they kept away from the car he was not bothered about them.

Nikolai was being honest when he told the nice Mrs Russell he was heading for Plymouth. Heading west and further away from his homeland, he hoped, would be an unexpected move by anyone chasing after him, because he knew if Roy Jasper survived he would identify his attacker as Russian. And they would expect him to head for the nearest port, probably Poole or even Weymouth, where he could steal a boat. From Plymouth, Volkov expected to work his passage back to Europe on a cargo ship.

But he needed to know first that Lodge was dead. He would never get another chance if he were to return to Russia after failing in what he saw as a justifiable mission. He knew his KGB bosses would need a lot of persuading but if he could convince them that Pyotr Petrovich's killer had been eliminated, he was sure of getting into their good books and back into action. He needed this to work; it was all he knew how to be!

Nikolai had studied his map well while staying at Mrs Russell's house and knew that if he kept to the minor roads crisscrossing the south and west of the country, it was for him the best way to avoid traffic cameras. He still considered stealing another car but that might draw attention to his plan and, besides, the little Datsun was behaving herself and driving well now that the oil problem was gone. It was just a bit small, Nikolai thought, for a good night's rest. He would have to decide tomorrow but, for now, she was all he had.

STEPHEN TELEPHONED SIR Geoffrey at home on his personal line. He brought him up to date with the fruitless search for Volkov but was able to tell him they were heading the right way, given the sighting in Burton Bradstock. He told Sir Geoffrey he would check out early in the morning and try to find Volkov at West Bay where he was reputed to be heading. Sir Geoffrey argued that they could be looking for a needle in a haystack, so he had another plan. They had discussed if before, Tiny Tim's idea had sparked it off, of Stephen becoming the bait rather than the cat chasing the mouse. Sir Geoffrey planned, he said, to put out a false message using the BBC radio news program to lure Volkov back by letting him know that Stephen Lodge was still alive.

"Of course, he might not listen to the News," Sir Geoffrey said, "in which case we are wasting our time, but I am relying on Volkov needing to know he has been successful in killing you before leaving the country."

"I need to draw him back onto familiar ground," said Stephen, "but are we not putting other people at risk, sir, if he returns to Ashfield? Would it be better to do the opposite and let him believe he has achieved his target."

"And put him back into the field as an active assassin? No, thank you. I want him dealt with, once and for all! I am going to send you to the countryside for recuperation. We have a safehouse in Chilcombe where we send foreign agents and persons of interest for interrogation. There is no one there at the moment, and it is not far from where you are now. The first radio report will be included on the eight o'clock news tomorrow morning, Saturday, so you have until then to pull the rabbit from the hat. After that time, if you have not caught the bastard, I want you to go to Chilcombe and wait for the mouse to come after the cheese."

"And then, sir?"

"Then the mouse gets caught in the trap and should not be expected to survive! I have already cleared it with the Minister of Defence and the Prime Minister. The Foreign Secretary will report the unfortunate loss of one of their countrymen to the Russian Embassy when we have completed our task but, if we are right and this is an unsanctioned mission, they will simply deny Nikolai Volkov's existence and do nothing."

"Dirty politics, sir?" said Stephen.

"Justice!" said Sir Geoffrey with a steely tone to his voice. "Justice for Roy Jasper, and for Jessica whom we nearly lost. For young Harri as well, following her abduction in '82 and the nice Mrs Smith who everyone, including you, told me about. Even for John Cartwright and that old man in Portsmouth!"

Stephen had never heard Sir Geoffrey speak in this manner before.

"We should have dealt better with Volkov when we had the chance!"

"His death wasn't sanctioned, sir," said Stephen.

"But his elimination is now, Stephen. It's time we put Nikolai Volkov to bed!"

"Yes, sir," Stephen was pleased but not smiling, "I agree. But if that doesn't work?"

"Make it work, man! If he makes a run for it, chase after him. Do whatever it takes to finish him off!" Sir Geoffrey slammed the phone down.

HARRI HAD SPENT the whole of Friday afternoon by her father's bedside at the Dorset County hospital with her mother. A second operation carried out on Wednesday was successful in stopping an internal bleed and now her dad was getting better. He was still unconscious, and he was wired up to monitors and respiratory pumps and all sorts of paraphernalia, but she had been allowed to sit with him, and she was happy that her friendly nurse, who was herself quite young, had taken such a supportive role in letting Harri be close to her father. She held his left hand, said her prayers, and prayed that he would come back to her and Mummy.

Sheila sat looking at her husband and watched her daughter's face anxiously. She did not think this was the right place for a nine-year-old to be and she did not want Harri to have these final memories of her father lying in a hospital bed, unable to do anything for himself. The medical equipment surrounding them frightened her and, despite what they had been told, she feared the worst for Roy. As she listened to Harri say her prayers, she accepted her daughter's faith was in hope while her own was in tatters.

Roy's left index finger twitched. Harri felt it. She looked at her mother and the pulse monitor spiked up. Her father's finger twitched again even as she held on to it, and her mother, with tears in her eyes, leaned against her little girl and gave her body a squeeze. Her young, friendly, nurse came into the room and picked up the other hand, checking for pulse against her watch. She gave them a thumbs-up.

"He's coming round," she said. "I'll get the doctor."

STEPHEN HAD WOKEN up and was checked out of the Anchor Inn at Burton Bradstock by 4 a.m. He drove the two miles to West Bay in under ten minutes and came into the seaside village via Station Road rather than turn toward Eype and Bridport first, That way would only bring him back again via the West Bay Road from Bridport. As he came around the bend formed by the Station Yard car park, he could see on his left a small red car standing alone in the East Beach car park. It was just beginning to get light. Another fine day was forecast.

Stephen was optimistic he had found the Russian but pulled into the Station Yard opposite as a precaution. He made sure his Walther PPK was armed and safely tucked away under his left arm. He might be licensed to carry but it was another thing entirely to use a gun or have it even on view in public on English streets. He did not like to use a gun anyway at short range, preferring the long shot that seemed less personal, but needs must. His only consoling thought was that he was protected by government sanction, so long as no innocent bystanders got hurt.

He stole across the empty road and approached the parked car from behind, drawing the Walther from its holster and slipping the safety switch to off. He knew the car's side mirrors might reflect his presence to the occupant, but he did his best to stay low. He identified the car as the stolen Datsun and expected to find Nikolai Volkov inside but was to be disappointed. He shuffled up the passenger side of the two-door hatchback and ripped the door open only to find it was empty!

NIKOLAI HAD ALREADY decided to change cars and

steal another one, which was made easy for him when he trawled the Bridport Arms car park by the pub of the same name and found a new Ford Escort with the doors unlocked. Even more stupid than that, the ignition keys were hidden in the glove compartment. How dumb can people be! The Ford was a standard four-door model, registration B140 JMV, and sea-green in colour.

It was only three o'clock in the morning and still night-time, so he drove the Escort around to East Beach and moved all his effects across to it, including his weapons, and said goodbye to the smaller Datsun. She had served him well and he accepted the car would be returned to her rightful owner in better condition than when he stole it, so long as a forensic examination didn't rip it to pieces. Getting away in the Ford Escort, which he was pleased to see had a full tank of petrol, he drove toward Bridport and turned left onto the A35 through Eype on the road to Lyme Regis. He would not travel any further west until he knew Lodge was dealt with.

STEPHEN WAS DISAPPOINTED by the empty Datsun and knew he would have to report it. That would take a few hours of his time and he decided he would have to accept the Chilcombe safe-house idea that Sir Geoffrey proposed. He put his own thoughts to one-side and shut the Datsun car door, going in search of a police station but quickly realising he would have to go to Bridport to find one, so he returned to his white Viva.

Bridport police were reluctant to get involved, especially as Stephen told them the car was legally ticketed until the end of the day. The police view was that the driver may well have returned already and driven off, so why waste police resources sending a car down there when they could be doing better work in Bridport. Stephen pointed out to them that they didn't seem to be doing any work in Bridport at all before he gave them Sir Geoffrey's MoD number and a police-sergeant put a call through.

The police-sergeant nodded at the telephone, said "Yes" and "No" a few times, and practically stood to attention as he concluded the conversation he was having.

"We'll send someone down there right away, sir!"

Stephen smiled at the desk-sergeant and said he'd be at the very convenient café next door to the station when they wanted him back.

"Do you have a road map I can borrow, please? I need to get to Chilcombe in the next couple of hours." He left to find a cup of coffee and some breakfast.

NIKOLAI WAS IN Lyme Regis, also having breakfast, when the eight o'clock news came on the radio. He asked for the volume to be turned up.

"A report has just come in of a spate of Ricin poisonings in Portsmouth over the last few weeks," said the news presenter. "An elderly man, thought to be an ex-Royal Navy seaman who takes in lodgers, has been found dead in his home, and we understand a young woman has also died in a London hospital following a visit to her boyfriend in Portsmouth. The police and local authorities are wondering if the young man, a Royal Navy lieutenant, had been targeted by the illegal immigrant community because of his Border Control work done on coastal patrol ships, and his girlfriend was an unfortunate bystander, but they cannot tie in the old sailor to that theory. The Naval lieutenant is said to be recovering and has been taken to Chilcombe House in Dorset, where he will convalesce before returning to duty. Police investigations are continuing."

Nikolai heard the report but did not want to believe his ears. Lodge? Alive? And where did they say he was going to? He asked a waitress when the news would be read again and was told that a short summary would be given at half past eight, so he waited but that only gave passing details and not the full story. Not wanting to draw attention to himself, he returned to the stolen car and sat in the car park listening to the radio while waiting for nine o'clock to come. The report was exactly the same as before. Chilcombe? Where was Chilcombe? He was sure he had seen it on the road map. He dug that out of his backpack to look at it. Stephen Lodge still alive? It could not be. It would not be. Nikolai would find Chilcombe, and he would deal with Lodge once and for all!

STEPHEN FINISHED HIS breakfast and went back into

the police station to be told that he would not be required any further, and his employer had left a message for him saying he should move on to his next port of call. Stephen offered to return the road map but was politely excused on the grounds they had plenty more. He had looked up Chilcombe while in the café and knew there were a couple of ways he could get there, deciding to go back through the Bride Valley rather than use the main A35. The sun was shining; it was about half past eight.

He drove back to Burton Bradstock via the Burton Road and on to Swyre on the B3157 coast road before turning left and left again to avoid Puncknowle, passing thatched cottages and farmers barns along the way. It was a beautiful day and he regretted not being able to enjoy it. He would love Jessica to see more of the countryside and realised he had not spoken to her since Thursday. He could only hope that this "safehouse" came with a telephone. Come to think of it, how was he going to get in? Sir Geoffrey hadn't told him that one.

Chilcombe was a lot smaller than Puncknowle, only a hamlet, but it had a church and the remains of a Tudor manor house, demolished in 1939. The largest cottage, Chilcombe House, was easy to find and Stephen was clearly expected by a caretaker chap who appeared as if from nowhere when he pulled up at the front. Stephen was directed indoors, and the kitchen, bathroom, and a telephone were all pointed out to him and said to be at his disposal, but would he please telephone Sir Geoffrey Cheeseman to say he'd arrived. He thanked the caretaker who placed the house keys on a side table. The caretaker said he would pick them up when Stephen left, and he was not to lock himself out.

"There's only ten of us live in Chilcombe as residents" he explained, "and we all work for the same employer, so we trust each other implicitly."

Stephen thanked him and waited for him to leave before taking his "tools" from the car to the house and having a look around. He needed to know which way Volkov would come if he does take the bait. He had heard the nine o'clock news and was impressed with the reporting. If Volkov also heard it he might be tempted, but Stephen had to prepare himself for a long wait. He decided he would have time to telephone Sir Geoffrey *and* Jessica while he did so.

Chapter 14

Cat and mouse

"Hello, Jessica, how are you," Stephen wished he were by her side but duty calls.

"Hello to you too. Where are you?" Jessica was bored. She wanted to be out of hospital and free.

"I can't tell you exactly," said Stephen, "if only because I'm not really sure. I am apparently the bait to catch the mouse that is Nikolai Volkov, but it's a bit of a shot in the dark because we don't exactly know where he is either and we can't be certain he will get the message that I am still alive. The only thing I am sure of is that he is still in the country and that he has been in West Bay recently."

"That pretty beach on the Dorset Coast? How I wish I were there right now. I'm going stir crazy in this hospital!"

"Still no better?" asked Stephen. "Still got fluid in the lungs?"

"Yes, but all the doctor is saying now is that I need to convalesce, and I have told him that I can do that just as well at home."

"You'll need someone to look after you. And I'm no bloody good stuck out here."

"Mum and Dad could come down," said Jessica. "We've got the spare room and they needn't stay forever, and I would love to get them out of my flat. They've got far too used to being there!"

"And when I'm done here," said Stephen regretfully, "they will be gone and I go back to the Navy, and who will look after you then."

"I will look after myself!" Jessica told him forcefully. "I would love it if people stopped prodding me about and telling me what to do and let me decide things for myself! I told you before, I'm a big girl now and I can make my own mind up on things. You, for instance. So what if you're away for a while? You'll come home eventually, and if you're gone overseas on a long tour, I will come with you, and we'll live in married quarters."

"For which, we will need to be married," said Stephen, knowing RN restrictions.

"If that's what it takes." Jessica told him.

Stephen thought carefully about his next words. "A telephone call is not how I would choose to propose to you."

"It's not *how* you propose to me, Stephen. It's *when*!"

They exchanged more pleasantries, told how they loved each other, and Stephen asked Jessica not to go back to the cottage until this business with the Russian was concluded. But Jessica said she would leave the hospital soon, so he had better hurry up!

The morning passed slowly. Stephen had found

food in the kitchen but wasn't interested. He only made himself a cup of coffee. He had a good look around the gardens and tried to second guess which way Volkov might make his approach. The cottage stood high on a hillside and there was only one road in, but Stephen thought the main road which bypassed the hamlet ran close by the side of Chilcombe House, so that was also a possibility.

He telephoned Sir Geoffrey after speaking with Jessica and confirmed all that had gone on with the red Datsun at West Bay and the police at Bridport. In return, Sir Geoffrey was able to tell him about another car, a new sea-green Ford Escort that had been reported stolen from the Bridport Arms car park overnight, and they both agreed that was probably Volkov. So, he knew what car to look for as well. The registration had been given to the traffic camera operatives to watch out for.

This setup was not what Stephen wanted. It was not his way, and he was uncomfortable with it, preferring to be the shooter rather than the target. As much as he could understand the need to lure Volkov out of hiding, he felt constrained by Sir Geoffrey's directions. Somehow or the other he hoped to lead Volkov onto more familiar territory but was unsure how to. It would mean leading him back to Ashfield and that was thirty miles away. He would have to pray that Volkov's obsession with revenge for Petrovich would obscure his common sense.

NIKOLAI STUDIED THE road map and saw he could approach Chilcombe quickest by returning east along the A35 road to Dorchester, but he could not go back through Bridport in case the police were already looking for the Ford Escort he had stolen overnight. So he took a long-winded route via minor roads to Broadwindsor and Beaminster, going close to Mapperton House and Uploders on the way to Loders Cross. As much as he was in a hurry, he needed to do what he could to avoid traffic cameras picking up the car. He did not want the police to pick him up before he could finish his mission. Driving carefully and keeping within the speed limitations, Mr Walker's road map was proving extremely useful in finding his way around, but he would have to scout the land carefully when he got to Chilcombe.

STEPHEN WORKED ON his guns, especially the Winchester rifle which had been stowed in his car for so long. A clean with a lightly oiled cloth sorted that out and he loaded the magazine although he didn't expect to use it. The Walther PPK was ready for use, and he kept that in his shoulder holster. He concluded his plan and made one more telephone call, thankful that he got through directly to the person he wanted to reach. All he could do now was wait.

He assumed an assault would have to be close range because Volkov would only have hand weapons, so Volkov's approach would come from the front of the cottage. He knew from the Roy Jasper attack his pursuer had a knife and guessed that he would be carrying a handgun. He would not have been able to hide anything else. In their line of work as contract killers, they were used to travelling fast, so light luggage was always small, a backpack or some such. They did carry sniper rifles when they were on a job, but these were usually collected covertly in the mission field, then left behind, and with Volkov being on an unsanctioned mission he would not have had the support or opportunity. Of course, Stephen realised that there were a lot of assumptions in his plan but that was all he had to work with. The front of the cottage looking down the gradient of the hillside was laid out as a shrubbed garden with plenty of trees, and this would offer cover to someone approaching from that direction. Stephen went upstairs and looked out over the garden from a front bedroom window, seeing that it gave him a better view, so he set his Winchester up where he could cover the grounds, unencumbered by leaving a window wide open on what was a very warm day. It was not his style to have to wait for someone coming after him; he preferred to attack, but he didn't even know if Volkov was going to show up.

VOLKOV *DID* IN fact have a rifle. He had found it in Moira Russell's garage while he was tidying up, hidden in a locked compartment below the work bench. It must have belonged to Mr Russell when he was alive, but there was only a small amount of ammunition. Every shot would have to count. It was not in the best of condition, having been hidden away so long, but Nikolai put it in the boot of the Datsun without Moira knowing and had managed to clean it up while on the road when he left Abbotsbury behind. He had not spoken of it to Mrs Russell, assuming she did not know about it. It wasn't the best of long-range weapons, but it could come in useful if the need arose. He assumed it had been used for shooting rabbits on their land but wasn't able to calibrate it because there had been no opportunity and not enough ammunition for practice shots.

He also had a small sniper's telescope. If he got a clear view of his target he thought he stood a chance, and the best opportunity for that was on the hillside rising from the back of Chilcombe House.

Nikolai had arrived at Chilcombe by eleven a.m. and parked the Ford Escort well into the side of the main road, partly assisted in hiding by the sea-green colour of the vehicle. He skilfully scouted the land around the house and knew he would be expected to approach from the front because it afforded the most cover. He crossed the downland to the north using sparsely grown trees as cover. He saw no other people and no other vehicles, the only sounds in the area were birdsong and the occasional bark of a dog, or maybe that of a fox. He identified Chilcombe House easily enough as there were very few properties in the hamlet: a church, the demolished manor house that still had its name emblazoned on a freestanding gatepost, a few smaller buildings. Patience was often the name of their game when they were on missions and Nikolai set himself up in a hollow on the hillside where he had a clear view of the house and smaller rear garden. He saw a person occasionally walk around the House grounds and using his sniper's telescope was confident it was Lodge but was too far away to be sure of the shot. Viewing the land between them, he spotted a tree that was closer and would provide sufficient cover for the task. It limited his sight of the house at ground level because of a low garden wall, but he might see someone in one of the windows.

THE FIRST SHOT missed Stephen, smacking into the house wall, scattering brick chips into the air! He had walked through to the back rooms occasionally just in case of a rear attack but did not really expect one so was caught off guard. He drew his pistol just as the second shot shattered the glass of the window he was looking through. He got off a couple of shots himself in the direction of the shooter but could not expect accuracy with a handgun at that range. It might just be enough to keep their head down.

NIKOLAI CURSED THAT he had been unable to calibrate the old rifle. He quickly adjusted and took a second shot which shattered the glass of the window, and he saw Lodge go down. He was not fooled however, and when gunfire was returned he knew that his target was still alive. Lodge must have used a handgun because his gunfire was inaccurate, but Volkov knew he would have to get closer for a kill-shot.

STEPHEN RAN BACK inside to fetch his rifle from the front window but then had an idea how to draw Volkov out. Ideally, he wanted to get him on the road in pursuit of his plan to take him away from Chilcombe and into more open country. Stephen accepted that his knowledge of the Bride Valley area was limited but he thought he knew what he could do. He ran downstairs and out into the back garden, keeping low just enough to be seen but not offering a clear target for Volkov to try a shot. Not that that stopped him. Volkov got off two more rounds that cannoned into the house wall behind him, and Stephen returned the fire wildly, wanting to arouse Volkov's ire and interest.

NIKOLAI WATCHED AS Lodge ran through the rear garden. Hampered by the low wall he took a couple of pot-shots hoping that Lodge would be drawn toward him but instead he seemed to be headed for his car. Was he going to make a run for it? Nikolai knew he had Lodge pinned down all the while he could keep him in the house and grounds, but he could not cover the front from where he was. He would need to block the driveway to prevent Lodge from leaving the house. He was running low on ammunition but took the old rifle with him and made a run for his car.

STEPHEN SAW VOLKOV break cover from his hiding place and tried a couple of shots with his Walther PPK, but the range was still too great. He guessed that Volkov's intention was to reach his car and block the driveway into the grounds or take off down the road. Stephen had changed his mind about teasing Volkov back towards Ashfield. It was just too far to expect to succeed, so he decided this should end now.

Quickly reaching his own car, Stephen revved it up and hurried down the drive and out of the village, leaving his rifle behind but blocking Chilcombe Lane just in time to stop Volkov getting away. The green Escort was coming straight for him as he vacated the Viva by sliding across the passenger side and levelled his gun at his enemy across the roof of the car, firing two shots directly at the windscreen. The Escort swerved into the high hedge at the side of the road as the windscreen shattered. Stephen stayed behind his own vehicle.

NIKOLAI SAW THE white car pull across the lane and cursed as he realised he was too late to block the driveway into the village. He saw Lodge stand up on the far side and the double flash as two shots were fired, swerving into the hedge on his right just as his windscreen shattered. So, if this was to be it, the final showdown between them, so be it! Nikolai drew his gun and fired not directly at Lodge but at his car. Two tyres were quickly blown out and then he turned his aim to the rear of the vehicle.

STEPHEN FELT THE car drop down as the two driver's side tyres were blown out by gunshot. Knowing what would come next he quickly ran backwards as the petrol tank was struck and the Vauxhall Viva, his Dad's pride and joy, blew up in a spectacular fireball that burned the trees and hedges on both sides of the lane. The boom from the explosion would be heard for miles around but, luckily, there were no other buildings affected. Stephen was blown further by the blast and bruised his body as he was thrown onto the metalled surface of the road.

NIKOLAI, SHELTERED BY the wreck of his own vehicle, watched the white car blow up and quickly ran past the ensuing fire to see what had happened to Lodge. He was disappointed not to find a charred body just beyond the ruined Viva.

STEPHEN HAD ROLLED to the left side of the road and rose to his knees just as Volkov came into sight on the right. He was in pain from the bruising he suffered as a result of the fireball but had not suffered any breakages or damage to his hands. He stood to face his enemy and called out to him from across the lane.

"You should not have returned, Mr Volkov," he shouted. Volkov stopped and looked in his direction.

"You killed my Pyotr," Volkov shouted back. "In Saigon, when you protected that worthless chemist, Con Trai Tốt. And we were all there to do the same thing: to prevent his work getting into the hands of the Chinese."

"I'm very sorry for your colleague, Mr Volkov," yelled Pyotr. "Had I realised what Con Trai Tốt was up to I would have completed the mission myself, but I was not fully aware."

"But Pyotr is dead, Mr Lodge, and for that you must die also. I am sorry also about your girlfriend, but Pyotr was the love of my life so it seemed only fitting that yours should die as well."

Stephen understood what Volkov was saying but asked the question anyway. "And what about the others?"

"Your friend Mr Jasper stopped me from killing you before, so he had to pay the price. As for the other two, they were both faggots and had served their purpose. You should be glad I took them off of your streets."

"And what are you? Are you not a faggot also?" Stephen hated using the term but was trying to goad Volkov into taking a shot. He could not just shoot him in cold blood; this was why he preferred his targets at the end of a sniper's rifle sight. This was too close, too personal.

"Are you not a homosexual also? Should I kill you

just for that? Did not those men deserve the freedom to live out their lives also."

"Pyotr and I were special!" Stephen could feel Volkov's anger rising. "We had been together for years. We were not fly by nights that trawled the streets or took men into our houses simply for the purpose of sex. We loved one another!"

Nikolai raised his gun, but Stephen was too quick for him to aim properly. Two bullets from the Walther caught him in the chest and he fell backwards. He was dead before he hit the ground.

SIR GEOFFREY CHEESEMAN did not mind working on a Saturday, although this was often done from home. From his point of view, with many of his operatives on mission around the globe, his role as coordinator was a twenty-four-hour job, seven days a week, and he loved it. His wife, Sarah, accepted she would always take second place to what her husband saw as his duty to Queen and Country even after he had left the Army, but she knew that so long as he had work he would remain strong and alive, and he was all she cared about. Retirement could wait for another ten years as far as she was concerned, but she knew he was under pressure for his post.

He took the call from Stephen at about ten a.m. to say that he was at Chilcombe, and promptly made another call to Blandford Camp, speaking directly to SB1 and SB2. He wanted them to proceed to Chilcombe straightaway but not to interfere unless they had to. They should stand ready at either end of Chilcombe Lane to stop the Russian escaping, should Stephen fail to do so. They should assume if the KGB man tried to leave the area, that Lodge was dead, and they had permission from the Minister of Defence to stop the Russian by whatever means.

Stephen Lodge, Sir Geoffrey knew, would not want to be hemmed in by Chilcombe House but it was necessary to have a location that Nikolai Volkov could find on a map to entice him out of hiding. He knew that his No 1 operative would not be able to draw Volkov into the familiar territory of Ashfield. It was just too far. He wanted the Russian dead and he wanted it done at Chilcombe where there were enough of their own people to clear up the mess. There was a rare risk he could be wrong, but that was the nature of their business.

STEPHEN STOOD OVER his enemy's body. He always regretted this moment: another person lost and at his hand, but that was the life he led. This one was more personal than all the others though. The death of Volkov would have to mark the end of his career as a contract killer. He felt it was time to hang up his gun and retire to the quiet life of the Dorset village he had chosen as home for himself and Jessica.

He was surprised when SB1 and SB2 showed up. Apparently, they had been contacted earlier by Sir Geoffrey to be the back-up should Stephen fail in his mission to stop Volkov. They had both been stationed about half a mile either end of the lane, one with their car at Rudge Farm to the south and the other one at the turning for Shipton Gorge to the north. When they heard the explosion of the Viva and saw the fireball go up, they both came running.

Residents from the village had also come running, including the caretaker of Chilcombe House. While one attended to Stephen who had begun to collapse from his bruising following the fire, others started to clear up the debris. A tractor appeared and chains were attached to the wreck of the Vauxhall, which was dragged up the driveway into the village. The Ford Escort, whose only damage bar a few scratches was the shattered windscreen, followed, driven by one of the villagers. Stephen watched open-mouthed as they efficiently and completely cleared up the lane until it was almost as if nothing had happened, the only evidence of which would be the scorched hedges and trees and they could be easily explained away, the caretaker told him.

SIR GEOFFREY TOOK the call just before his one o'clock lunch.

"The job is done, sir," said the caretaker. "The Russian has been eliminated and his body awaits collection from the house."

"And Mr Lodge?" asked Sir Geoffrey anxiously.

"Suffering from bruises but otherwise unhurt. The Special Branch will escort him back to Blandford

Camp. I'm afraid his own car suffered a catastrophic fire."

"Then thank goodness he was not in it at the time," said Sir Geoffrey. "What about the other car?"

"In remarkably good condition all things considered," said the caretaker. "The windscreen's shattered and there is glass debris inside and a few scratches out, but we can get that sorted easily enough, and then it can go back to its owner as a retrieved vehicle via the police. No one needs to know more. Same arrangements as before?"

"Oh, yes," said Sir Geoffrey, "It will cost us a bit, but just bill the MoD in the usual way."

"Thank you, sir."

"And thank you. I will arrange for a coroner's wagon to pick up the body. Please ask Mr Lodge to call me when he gets back to Blandford Camp, or home."

When Sir Geoffrey had concluded that call he had to make a few more, including to the Minister of Defence and the Foreign Secretary, and the BBC, but they could wait. Lunch first, he thought, and a well-earned double brandy.

EDDIE WAITED WITH his friends on Ashfield Hill. His was the third call that Stephen had made that morning. His instructions were clear: somehow or the other Stephen wanted him to block the road to a particular car travelling into or out of Ashfield between three thirty and four thirty that Saturday afternoon. Easier said than done but Eddie was a resourceful seventeen-year-old with friends who welcomed a bit of adventure on an otherwise empty weekend. Two other boys had recently acquired motor scooters like his as a reward for completing school, and three girls turned up on their bicycles in response to his telephone calls.

"What are you up to?" his mother, Jane, had asked, not knowing about the call from Stephen Lodge.

"I'm meeting some mates up by the Bike Park and we're gonna test out their skills on their new scooters."

Jane was taken in by the idea that her rather introverted son was getting out and about and mixing with others.

And so they waited, the boys driving up and down and around the hill, sometimes giving their female friends a pillion ride on the back of their scooters. Eddie hadn't told them the real reason for what they were doing, just that they were going to have an hour or so's fun on their bikes. A few vehicles came by but nothing that matched the description Stephen had given him. To be honest, he was a bit disappointed, but it was probably just as well.

Chapter 15

All's well ...

Sir Geoffrey and Lady Sarah Cheeseman always watched the television together on Saturday nights if they were not attending some function or the other.

"This is the nine o'clock news on the BBC. I'm Mary Stewart. News is just coming in of an incident today resulting in the death of a man thought to be responsible for the Ricin poison deaths that have occurred over the past few weeks in Portsmouth and London. Special Branch officers were sent to Chilcombe in Dorset where one of the victims of the poison is recovering, to arrest the man whom police had been searching for, believed to be a rogue Russian KGB agent. After a car chase on narrow country lanes, the dead man's car spun out of control before catching fire. The Russian Embassy in London have been contacted by the BBC but have declined to comment. Other news tonight ..."

Moira Russell had also watched the news on the television, and remembered it was the one obsession of her recent lover, that he would listen to all the news programmes. She knew in her heart that it was Pyotr Petrovich they were reporting about but despite all that he was said to have done, she still felt sorrow for the Russian man who had behaved impeccably well at her house this past week and had given her such pleasure with his company.

AFTER THE CLASH with Nikolai Volkov, Stephen had been driven to Blandford Camp by SB1 and SB2. He mourned the loss of his father's Vauxhall Viva but was thankful to have survived the explosion of the petrol tank. At the camp, he was treated in their sickbay for his bruises and one or two scratches, but he was otherwise okay. The Special Branch officers took a full statement from him at the same time as telling him about the set up at Chilcombe and how the residents of the hamlet were all trained "for incidents like this." Stephen asked them to pass on his thanks.

SB1 took Stephen home to his cottage where he could see that Tony Woods had made a good start on the garage extension but still had a lot to do. Stephen knew that he would have to rent or buy another car but thought that Albert's Morris Minor would get him around for the time being. He knew he should contact Sir Geoffrey but decided to leave it until the following morning. He would go up to London on Monday and see about bringing Jessica home to Dorset. If he could not persuade her doctors, he felt sure the Foreign Secretary could. Tomorrow he would remind Tiny Tim at the Greene Dragon of his promise to throw the bar open on news of the Russian's death, but also to celebrate Stephen's birthday. He was thankful to have kept that quiet until now.

He did not sleep well, going over the whole business in his mind, the people who had suffered, the lives lost, including Volkov and his parents, and all because of the work that he chose to be party to. He resolved yet again to retire from the business and settle back into Royal Navy life with a promise to work hard at the Maritime Warfare School and gain promotion to Lieutenant Commander. He would enjoy a spell of shore-based stability at HMS Vernon if they would have him back, where he had enjoyed teaching boys hardly out of school age, just like he had been years before, keen young recruits who wanted to learn about Ops. Room procedures.

But first he would give thanks at church and there, with Jane's help, he could meet and make his peace with Sheila Jasper. He looked forward to seeing Harri and to hear how her father was doing. It had only been two or three days but so much had happened it seemed much longer. He walked up early to St Joseph's, thankful for the continuing sunny weather, and sat for a long while at the tomb of Hilda Smith, buried next to her beloved husband Albert, explaining all that had happened and how he would make her home alive again. He resolved to light a candle in her memory but also to light a second one for Nikolai Volkov. At the end of the day, Stephen thought, he was a man much like me, another circumstantial but tragic loss.

ROY JASPER WAS able to sit up in his hospital bed. It had been two weeks since the assault by Nikolai Volkov and a week since he came round from his surgery. He was told he had lost one kidney which was too severely damaged by the knife attack and that this could result in higher blood pressure and fluid retention in the future. The biggest effect it would have on him would be to cut out alcohol. He couldn't see himself managing that. Surely, one pint a week in the Greene Dragon wouldn't hurt. Perhaps, he thought, if he made it a habit to visit the pub straight after church on Sundays, the Good Lord could lend a helping hand?

Sheila had come to the hospital every day, shutting the shop for the afternoon, but his daughter Harri had been sent back to school this past week. It was the end of the summer term soon and they did not want her to miss out on the fun. He loved them both and understood how difficult this last two weeks had been for them. Some adjustments would need to be made to their lifestyle, but Roy had been told he should be back to work before the end of August. The leader of Bristol City Council where Roy worked, and the mayor of Bristol had both been in to see him and assured him that his job was safe, and they looked forward to his return.

He'd had one other visit in the middle of the

week by Stephen Lodge and had been told about Volkov's death. Roy already knew what work Lodge did outside of the Navy so was not surprised at the news. He was relieved that the Russian had been dealt with and hoped they could all enjoy a more peaceful life in Ashfield village now. Of course, he was disappointed to have missed the celebration when Tim Marshall threw open his bar last Sunday, but in his present condition he couldn't have enjoyed himself anyway.

STEPHEN KNEW THAT he would soon have to return to the Royal Navy but had been granted an extension to the Easter leave that had been so taken up by the Yvonne Fletcher tragedy and the Tripoli mission. He had been up to London and persuaded Jessica's doctors that she could return home to Ashfield, where her parents would continue to look after her when he was elsewhere. He had enjoyed his birthday on the previous Sunday, speaking at length to Jessica on the telephone, telling her of his plan to bring her home, and calling Sir Geoffrey Cheeseman to arrange a meeting in his London office for the Monday morning. Tiny Tim had thrown his bar open as promised, advertising for new custom from around the village on the back of celebrating Stephen's birthday. Only the two of them knew the real reason for the celebration.

He went to the North Dorset Railway station on Sunday afternoon to see Eddie and thank him for his actions the day before. His mother, Jane, was not best pleased at what Stephen had asked her son to do, but Stephen had been impressed by the lad's resourcefulness at getting his mates to help. He told Eddie what his own plan had been and why it didn't happen and took the opportunity once again to press him on giving a career with the Royal Navy further thought. Eddie rewarded him by saying he would discuss it with his dad when Eric came home at the end of the week.

Stephen had made his peace with Sheila Jasper and rejoiced with Harri at the news that her father was awake and recovering in the Dorset County Hospital. He resolved to visit during the week, with Sheila's permission, and was pleased to lift Roy's spirit with the news about Volkov and assured Roy that the whole village awaited his return.

STEPHEN STEPPED INTO Sir Geoffrey's office early on Monday morning and was greeted with a hug and a welcome cup of coffee by Hazel Eaves, Sir Geoffrey's secretary. She wanted to know how Jessica was and when she would get out of the hospital and was pleased when Stephen told her he would taking her home today. Sir Geoffrey asked how he could be so certain the doctors would sign her discharge.

"That's when you come in, Sir Geoffrey. I would ask you to telephone your contacts in the Foreign Office and ask them to apply pressure on the hospital that one of their top employees would heal quicker if she were allowed to do so at home. Then she can return to her duties in the Foreign and Commonwealth Office."

"I can see you are learning, lad," Sir Geoffrey responded warmly. "We'll get this debrief over and then I'll make a few calls. I have something else I want to discuss with you but that can wait until the dust has settled. Speaking of settling down, have you thought any more of that other matter we discussed?"

"I have, sir," Stephen smiled, "and I think you might have been prompting Jessica a little as well."

"Aah well," Sir Geoffrey shrugged. "It takes two to make a decision like that."

THEY DISCUSSED THE whole of the Volkov case, and Stephen told Sir Geoffrey of his plan to retire from the business. His boss was not surprised but asked Stephen to hold his horses until they could have another discussion later in the summer. He also told Stephen that Captain Husband looked forward to his return to HMS Vernon when the new "school" year commenced on the 3rd of September, and Stephen would be left alone with no further calls to duty until then so that he and Jessica could both fully recover and settle into their new life together. Stephen asked about the Warfare Officer training and his possible promotion to Lieutenant Commander, which had suddenly become more important to him, and was told that if he worked hard his promotion was guaranteed but not until he had completed an academic year at HMS Vernon, i.e., July next year.

"HEY," SAID STEPHEN as he greeted Jessica with a kiss and a fresh bunch of flowers purchased from the stall outside the hospital. She wished him a belated happy birthday and apologised for the lack of a birthday card. Her parents were there also, and he greeted them with a handshake for Dad and a kiss on the cheek for Mum. Stephen said he was going to talk with the doctors about Jessica's discharge at the same time as telling her they would need her car to get back to Ashfield as his was written off in an accident.

"Your dad's Viva?" Jessica was alarmed. "He would not be happy."

"What happened, Stephen?" asked her father, being more practical. Jessica's parents had no idea about Stephen's work other than being in the Royal Navy.

"I'm getting a bit old for the boy racer image," explained Stephen, guardedly. "I was having a race with myself around some narrow Dorset country lanes and took a corner too fast. The car rolled into a hedge and has been deemed irreparably damaged by the car's insurers."

"And you won't get any compensation because you caused the accident yourself?" more a statement by Jessica's father than a question.

"That's correct," said Stephen mournfully, and told them that he was using Albert's Morris Minor just to do local journeys, one of which was to drive up to Sherborne Station for the train that morning.

"I hope you'll take better care of Jessica's car," said her father, and they all laughed because they knew Jessica would never allow anyone else to drive it.

THEY LEFT THE hospital at four p.m. intending to go back to Jessica's flat and stay the night before driving down to Ashfield the following day. Sir Geoffrey had made the call and the Foreign Secretary no less had telephoned the hospital to request the return of his "favourite secretary." The doctors could not raise a plausible objection and Jessica was discharged but told to continue resting for at least another two weeks. Mum and Dad had agreed to return to her flat earlier to organise their stuff and vacate, returning home before the end of the day. Dad had raised a concern about their daughter, but Mum said they should "leave the kids to get on with their lives." Dad agreed so long as he could visit Ashfield before the end of the month and they made a date for Sunday, the 29th of July.

Jessica was glad to get out of the hospital. She knew what Stephen had been going through and insisted that he told her everything while they ate dinner at a small bistro near her flat. She had not previously been listening to the television or radio news, so she knew nothing of the Chilcombe incident. She understood how he felt about losing his dad's car but was thankful because he had not been in it when Volkov blew it up.

The next morning they drove to Ashfield, Jessica insisting as usual that she would drive. One of the first places they visited in the village was the Greene Dragon, where she personally thanked Tiny Tim Marshall with a kiss for helping Stephen celebrate his birthday. They walked around to St Joseph's to see the Vicar but, although the door was unlocked, Reverend James St Johns was not to be found. Perhaps he was at the school: they knew he went there frequently to take assembly and to sit in on Religious Education lessons.

Sheila Jasper was very relieved to see Jessica returned to the village when she came back from her afternoon visit to see Roy, and readily agreed to Stephen's planned visit to Roy the next day. She implored Jessica to stay at the Store until Harri came home from school and the little nine-year-old was equally excited to see her, giving her such a squeeze that it took Jessica's breath away. There were tears and laughter in equal measure and Stephen explained that both of them would be staying in the village for several weeks until Jessica was fully recovered, and Stephen went back to the Royal Navy, but that Jessica and he would return at weekends to continue doing Farthing Corner House up and start work on the front garden which was, they admitted, "a bit of a mess."

LIFE IN THE village settled down, and Stephen and Jessica settled in as a couple. Eddie Kemp came to visit about a week later with his father to explain to Stephen how they had talked his future through and that an apprenticeship in the Navy was something they both felt could be beneficial. Stephen was pleased and said that he would find out what was involved in the application process and report back but suggested that Eddie should enjoy his first post-school summer which, weather-wise, was a glorious one and maybe get a job to help his finances. Eddie chuckled, telling Stephen how he already had one: helping Farmer Tom Walker with his cattle and sheep and renovating some of the old machinery on Fennel Farm.

Church had become a big part of their life together. Stephen had always participated, remembering his days in the youth fellowship at St Mark's in Gillingham, Kent, but it was a new experience for Jessica although she quickly found that it was a good way to catch up on village gossip. They met Ted and Mavis Jarvis at St Joseph's and Stephen was able to thank Ted for his part in saving Roy Jasper. The retired ambulance driver, a gentle soul his wife insisted, was overly modest about his actions that night and said it could have gone so wrong. But the couple had since become surrogate carers for little Harri, who sometimes got out of school before her mother got home from the hospital.

Tony Woods, the garage builder, kept to his word and completed his work before the end of August. They were congratulated by their neighbours for how well the new garage blended in. Stephen took Jessica down to Blandford Forum and withdrew the money needed to pay off the builder from their local bank account, arranging at the same time for another transfer of money from their main account in London.

ROY JASPER RETURNED from hospital on Sunday the 12th of August, collected by his wife and daughter in their car. He had been in the Dorset County for more than a month and was still not fully fit, but the doctors allowed him to convalesce at home. When he got together with his neighbour Jessica, they agreed that their status as "war-wounded" meant they deserved to be waited on hand and foot by their families but that didn't really work for Sheila and Stephen, although Harri did her best to welcome her father home.

The Vicar paid a pastoral visit to both families and Stephen spoke with him about maybe telling Joan Cartwright how John had really died, but James St Johns counselled that there was no gain to Joan to know the awful truth that her brother was murdered, so Stephen let the idea pass.

STEPHEN AND JESSICA enjoyed being in the village, the smallness and quietness of it, but knew that by the end of the month they would return to their respective jobs. For Jessica this would mean going back to live in the city most of the time, but she felt she had the best of both worlds now, concerts, plays, and dinner dates with friends in the big city while enjoying the idyllic weekends at their country retreat as she saw it. It was on one of those "idyllic weekends" that Stephen finally got around to pop the question she had been hoping for, for years. She had loved this man from the get-go four years previous but knew that, in his head, his work had always got in the way.

"Let's take a run to Golden Cap," Stephen said to her over their Saturday breakfast. The garage work was almost finished, just the doors to be moved from the old to the new front entrance, a job that Tony Woods asked Stephen to help them with, and he, Stephen, had asked them to take the weekend off because he would "be away with the girlfriend."

"Where's Golden Cap?" asked Jessica, finishing off her eggy-soldiers, one of her favourite childhood breakfasts and one she still enjoyed having been reintroduced to her during her recent hospital stay.

"It's a high hill just past West Bay and has a great panoramic view of the Jurassic Coast. It's the highest point and has views over Lyme Bay to the west and Chesil Beach to the east. I am told that on a good day you can see right across Torbay to the Start Point lighthouse south of Dartmouth, and today is a gloriously sunny day."

"And how are we supposed to get there," said Jessica. She had learned some of her practicality from her father. "It sounds like a long drive and

I'm not sure I'm up to that yet. And you haven't got your new car yet."

Stephen had ordered a new silver Mazda 626, which would not arrive until the end of August.

"Let's take the Morris?" suggested Stephen. "It will be a bit slow, but it will be fun, and I've never given her a real run-out so it's a great opportunity to do so."

"Is it easy to get to, this ... Golden Cap?" asked Jessica, sceptical about whether Albert's Morris Minor would get them there *and* back.

"Yes," said Stephen, finishing the cup of coffee he had made twenty minutes prior to breakfast and realising it was a bit cold now. "Up Ashfield Hill and over Tolworth to Winterbourne Whitechurch, then along the A354 to Puddletown and the A35 the rest of the way. And, if you're particularly good, we can stop at Dorchester for a meal on the way home."

"Okay," she laughed, "but you'll have to drive. I'm not familiar enough with Albert's car anyway," that was how they liked to refer to it, " and I might get too tired."

They cleared up after breakfast and were on the road by ten o'clock. Stephen reckoned on an hour and a half to get to Langdon Hill on the side of Golden Cap.

"I was tempted by West Bay, but I think it would be too much of a climb for you to walk from there and Langdon Hill is just off the A35," said Stephen. "Golden Cap and Langdon Hill are National Trust properties and it's a gentler gradient from the car park at Langdon to the top of Golden Cap. It might be blowy with a breeze off the English Channel so take a headscarf, but I think it's going to be a warm day."

And that was what they did. The drive was lovely, and the car ran remarkably well and was wonderfully comfortable. As they pulled into Langdon Hill car park, Stephen noted the time was not yet half past eleven. He was glad they had brought a vacuum flask for coffee, although Jessica preferred water for herself. The sun shone and it was warm and the walk to the Cap was not steep but was still up-hill. Jessica was soon puffing as he held her hand and guided her along the pathways: at first, a shaded wood path and then through a few gates and across two fields to get to the Golden Cap viewpoint.

By the time they got there Jessica needed to sit down but there were no benches, so they sat on the grass. Golden Cap is so called because of its sandy soil and the colour, glowing in the warm sun, matched the East Beach cliffs they could see to the east beyond West Bay. The pundits were right, and you could see the eighteen-mile stretch of Chesil Beach all the way along the coast to the faint outline of Portland Bill in the distance. To the west, Stephen could see across the Lyme Bay but struggled to see to the other side of Torbay clearly enough to be sure of Start Point, or even Brixham where his mate Terry still lived, although Terry had now returned to duty, so he'd heard.

Stephen and Jessica sat on the grass together and stood up occasionally to go across to the barrier fence before the cliff face to enjoy the views. It was on one of these occasions that Stephen lifted Jessica up to sit atop the fence while he clumsily searched his pockets for the right one.

"I'm not very good at this sort of thing," he said, standing in front of her and excusing himself. "But, I wondered if you, Jessica, would do me the honour of becoming my wife?" and he held out his right hand, where a small golden ring sat, mounted by a large diamond.

Jessica looked at him with a feeling of joy in her heart and a tear in her eye, but she wanted the full proposal. Stephen eventually got the message and lowered himself on one knee, and Jessica stood down from the fence, holding his left hand with her right.

"Jessica Thomson," said Stephen, once again holding up the pretty engagement ring. "Will you marry me?"

Jessica offered her left hand as she said "Yes" and was impressed with the perfect fit as Stephen slid the ring onto her third finger.

"Of course I will," she said pulling him up so that she could kiss him, long, and hard. "And I will follow you wherever your journey takes you, Stephen Lodge, whatever the future holds."

They held onto each other for a long time afterwards and walked slowly back to the car.

From there, they could drive back to The George in Dorchester and enjoy a late lunch of pie and chips, emulating the very first meal they had enjoyed together in London when they met exactly four years earlier on the 25th of August 1980. Jessica hadn't remembered the significance of the date, but Stephen clearly had. She was impressed with the thoughtful romance of the occasion. They couldn't decide how long it would be before they actually got married but they knew where ... at St Joseph's in Ashfield, and all their friends would have to come and visit the village they now called home.

STEPHEN HAD ONE more job to do before he went back to his Royal Navy duties. He helped Tony Woods on the Monday, which he realised was Bank Holiday and went up to town by train on Tuesday. He had written his resignation letter on Sunday after they had been to church and everyone congratulated them on their engagement, the women especially wanting to see the new ring on Jessica's finger. Stephen was going to see Sir Geoffrey Cheeseman for a private luncheon, and Jessica took the opportunity to go to London to discuss her wedding plans with some of her girlfriends.

"It's good to see you, Stephen," said Sir Geoffrey, over a small lunch of ham and salad. "I hope you've had a satisfactory break?" referring to Stephen's long leave.

"Yes. Thank you, sir," replied Stephen, "and I'm

ready to go back to work, with the Navy. But before we go on, I just wanted you to know that I have proposed marriage to Jessica, and she has accepted. It will be a while before the wedding, certainly not this year, but I am happy to have taken your advice."

"Well, congratulations. A toast; to the happy couple!" and he raised his rather full brandy glass to chink Stephen's white wine.

"Thank you," said Stephen with a big schoolboy's smile on his face. "I wanted to ask if you would do me the honour of being my best man?"

"Oh," Sir Geoffrey was caught by surprise. "But don't you think you would rather have someone more your own age, lad. After all, there's almost thirty years between us."

"And you have known me for more than fifteen of them," replied Stephen. "I don't really have anyone that close in my own age group, except for Terry Salt, and I'm not sure I could put that kind of pressure on him. He's only just got back to work after his breakdown over the Falklands. And as you know only too well, I'm not the greatest of mixers outside of our small group."

"No, I guess not," said Sir Geoffrey, warming to the task ahead. "And Lady Sarah will be tickled at this old man being somebody's best man at a wedding, a post that I have never been asked to fill before. I shall be incredibly happy and honoured to accept your invitation." And he stood to shake Stephen by the hand and chink glasses once again.

"But that is not my only reason for seeing you today, Sir Geoffrey," Stephen started. "I have come to give you my formal resignation from the Special Task Group. I can no longer fulfil my duties as a Stag." And he handed across an envelope containing his resignation letter.

"I know, lad, I know," Sir Geoffrey said, taking the envelope and placing it carefully in his inside pocket without opening it. "And I accept. This Volkov business really shook you up, I could see that, and you'll have family to look after now."

"But, before you disappear completely, I want you to hear me out." Sir Geoffrey sat back in his chair and studied Stephen's emotions as he spoke to him. "As you know, I have been fighting for the past year against those in the Ministry who think I'm getting too old for this job. Well, now we've reached an arrangement. I would prefer to have gone on to my grave, but Lady Sarah has said it's time I hung up my boots and we settled down to the quiet life of golf on Wednesdays and Saturdays, and accept the occasional invitation to a formal do, if only so that she can buy new clothes and dress up posh."

"She's tired, lad. And, truth be told, so am I. I have agreed with the current Minister of Defence and the Prime Minister, bless her, that I will retire before my seventy first birthday, and that gives me just two and a half years to train my successor. And I would like that to be you, Stephen."

Stephen's mouth fell open. "Me, sir? But I'm not

very experienced at your level. I don't have the rank to command the Group."

"It's not about rank, Stephen, it's about ability. And you have that in abundance. I didn't get my knighthood for what I do here, or for the contacts that I have elsewhere. It has more to do with my military standing, but when I left the Army I needed a job, so I applied for this one and got lucky. You might not have realised it, Stephen, but you were my first STaG and have been with me all the way through."

"But I still don't have the rank, sir," Stephen was trying to persuade his boss of the mistake he could be making.

"You'll be a Lieutenant Commander soon, and a Captain, I'll bet, before you leave the Navy. But leave you will, and you've only got three years to serve and then you'll be looking for work. You might not have the contacts that I've got but I can introduce you to them, and it won't take much effort on their part to look upon you favourably as my replacement. It's not a given, but I think they can be persuaded to accept your application for the post."

"Well, sir," said Stephen, stunned by the opportunity. "But any application by me will have to wait at least a year. I have an obligation to Captain Husband at HMS Vernon to complete at least one academic year, and you and I have a wedding to arrange."

Sir Geoffrey smiled because Stephen had not said no to the job. "And I shall take advantage of you being shore-based and start to make some of those introductions.

"Thank you, sir," said Stephen.

THE END.

POSTSCRIPT:

NIKOLAI VOLKOV SENT one message to his KGB bosses during his time in England. He hoped it would elevate his standing with them. It concerned the recognition of a resident in Ashfield whom he knew was on their "Most Wanted" list: Jakub Havel from Czechoslovakia, otherwise known as the Vicar of St Joseph's, the Reverend James St Johns.

APPENDIX:

Characters

- Month and Year – April to August 1984.
- The place -- Ashfield village, nestled into the Dorset hills between Blandford Forum and Sturminster Newton.
- The village pub – The Greene Dragon
- Stephen's cottage – Farthing Corner House

- Stephen Lodge – Lieutenant, Royal Navy, member of a Special Task Group, STaG, under the Ministry of Defence. Stephen is thirty-six years old. and his birthday is on the 15th of July. He loves living in the village of Ashfield where he has bought Farthing Corner House after the death of Mrs Hilda Smith.

- Harriet (Harri) Jasper – is a bright and excitable girl of nine and a half years of age, who lives at the Jasper's General Stores in Ashfield village that is run by her mother. Her birthday is the 10th of October. Harri is an only child and attends the village primary school, where she has a reputation for fanciful stories and a vivid imagination. Harri was abducted by Nikolai Volkov just after her eighth birthday.

- Sheila Jasper – is Harri's mother and owner of the general store. Sheila is thirty, happy enough in her work, and loves living in the village of Ashfield, despite not being a "local." Sheila was born and raised on a huge suburban estate in Bristol but hated the hustle and bustle of city life. Running the local General Stores in Ashfield is her way of doing something "in the community" of Ashfield.

- Roy Jasper – Sheila's husband, and Harri's father. Roy works for Bristol City Council as a senior accountant and commutes for two hours each way to and from the office. He has learned to enjoy life in Ashfield, especially following his daughter's abduction eighteen months ago, when he decided to shorten his working week to four days a week.

- Plain Jane – or Mrs Jane Kemp: mum to twins Paul and Peter, a year younger than Harri, and Eddie who is in his final year at school and hoping for an apprenticeship in Blandford Forum. Jane's husband, Eric, works away on North Sea oil rigs, and she runs a tearoom at the former North Dorset Railway station.

- The Reverend James St Johns – fifty-nine years of age, whose real name is Jakub Havel and is of Czech origin. James has been the vicar of St Joseph's for about twenty-five years and is well liked in the village but is very private about himself.

- Timothy Marshall – Landlord of the Greene Dragon pub, Not-So-Tiny-Tim to customers and friends that knew him well. Ex-Army, six foot seven and over three hundred pounds, Tim is not to be tangled with. Every time he hits his head on the low wooden beams in his country pub he etches the date into the wood where it happened before covering it with a padded cushion. There are a lot of people glad of those fenders as they walk about the old country pub.

- Jessica Thomson – Stephen's girlfriend, who works as a secretary at theForeign and Commonwealth Office. Vivacious, red-haired, and very much in love with Stephen, Jessica has her own apartment in London and is thirty-one years old. Her birthday is the 29th of November.

- Sir Geoffrey Cheeseman – Stephen's boss. Sir Geoffrey has worked for Her Majesty's government for many years, both in the military and post-retirement from the Army. His final rank was Lieutenant-Colonel, but he prefers to be addressed by his much-deserved knighthood. Sir Geoffrey is now sixty-eight years old, married to Lady Sarah Cheeseman, and facing compulsory retirement. He heads up the Special Task Group for the Ministry of Defence.

- Hazel Eaves – Sir Geoffrey Cheeseman's secretary. Hazel is mid-forties and has been a civil servant all her working life. She is a single woman without children but does not regret her dedication to her work, and especially to the unusual work of Sir Geoffrey's office.

- The Vauxhall Viva SL – Stephen swapped his father's car for his own Ford Capri at the start of 1982. Stephen keeps his father's car protected by a tarpaulin at Farthing Corner House, Ashfield, but hopes soon to have a new garage.

- Nikolai Volkov – Russian KGB agent bent on revenge for the death of his colleague and lover Pyotr Petrovich, who was shot and killed by Stephen Lodge while on a mission in Saigon in 1982. Nikolai abducted Harri Jasper in an attempt to lure his target into his sights but was thwarted and arrested.

- Lieutenant Commander Duncan Robson – Captain of HMS Alderney, and Stephen's commanding officer. Captain Robson is a traditionalist and enjoys Naval life. He likes detail and truth.

- Sub Lieutenant Jordan Scott – junior officer on HMS Alderney.

- Leading Seaman Andy Williamson – quartermaster and senior-helmsman on HMS Alderney. Andrew Williamson from Wales is a three-badge leading hand in the Royal Navy, having served fourteen years and just signed up for his final draft which would take him to compulsory retirement at the age of forty-four, unless he can seal a commission before then.

- Jack Milligan – skipper of the MV Rosamund Queen, a fishing vessel now used as a diving boat in Scapa Flow.

- Chris Milligan – Jack's son.

- Peter J. Fellowes – a visitor from Canada wanting to scuba dive in Scapa Flow "just for the experience."

- Reg Cornall and Dave Clements – fellow scuba enthusiasts and friends of Peter Fellowes.

- Able Seaman Joe Hall – Cox for Alderney's whaler boat.

- John Bell – nicknamed Dinger in keeping with Naval traditions, is a Leading Seaman on HMS Alderney with a specialisation of "Diver."

- Sidney Saunders – an Able Seaman and another qualified Diver on the Alderney.

- Robert Ford and Ian Brown – two "Stags" working for Sir Geoffrey Cheeseman.

- Mustafa Ahmed – a Libyan terrorist suspected of killing WPC Yvonne Fletcher.

- Oliver Miles – Her Majesty's Ambassador to Libya.

- Ms Teresa Parker – Planning office manager for Dorchester District Council.

- Mr John Turner – Dorset County surveyor seconded to the Dorchester DC planning office.

- John Cartwright – Teacher, Ashfield C of E Primary School. John, who is fifty-one and grossly overweight, is affectionately known as Haystack by his pupils due to his mass of unruly hair. John has died suddenly during the Easter school holiday.

- Simon Anchorman – headmaster of Ashfield Church of England Primary School.

- Joan Cartwright – sister of the unfortunate John, who lives in Sturminster Newton.

- Miss Susan Sandhurst – junior partner at Able Architects.

- Commodore D.C. Lewis – commanding officer of HMS Nelson in 1984.

- Captain Brian Moss – executive officer at HMS Nelson n 1984.

- Captain Jonathan D.W. Husband – commanding officer of HMS Vernon in 1984.

- Johnny "Jack" Johnston – an old faggot living in Portsmouth. An ex-Royal Navy seaman, now nearly seventy, Jack gives lodgings to Nikolai Volkov in return for certain "favours."

- Ted and Mavis Jarvis – Ashfield residents. Retiree Ted rescued Roy Jasper when he was attacked by Nikolai Volkov.

- SB1 & SB2 – two Special Branch officers sent to Blandford Camp by Sir Geoffrey Cheeseman.
- Police-Sergeant Ronald Blake – based at Ashdown.

- Thomas Walker – farmer, owner of Fennel Farm, formerly "Smiths."

- Tony Woods – sole proprietor of Extraordinary Woods, the company contracted to build Stephen and Jessica's garage extension.

- Mrs Moira Russell – who befriends Nikolai Volkov. Moira is sixty-two and lives with James, her black Highland Terrier, near the Hardy Monument on Black Down.

About the Author

KEITH SALTER (FORD) is seventy-five years old and now lives in Southampton, England, having originated from Gillingham, Kent. Frustrated with life following his enforced retirement after twenty years of working as a retail clerk for the local railway, he has watched unwittingly as his small retirement nest egg has dwindled away. The COVID-19 pandemic of 2020 prevented his intention to return to work in a part-time capacity, and now ill-health and minor disabilities stop him from doing so.

In 2021, Keith self-published a two-volume autobiography that revealed his somewhat chequered past in the hope that it would set the record straight and he could find a level of acceptance amongst his peers. To an extent, it worked, but not without uncovering abuse within his own family that could and should have been dealt with years before.

Keith identifies as a Christian but is not a regular attendee at Church. He finds piety to be a poor substitute for charitable action. It has taken him years to come to terms with the forgiveness of God for his own dark past, but he believes he is now at the foot of the Cross rather than still in death's valley.

In 2022, Keith rediscovered a list of six book outlines he had written thirty-five years previously. Always aspiring to be a published author, he began to write a short series of stories based around a Royal Naval officer, Stephen Lodge, and that is how the Lodge Looks Back series was born.

Printed in Great Britain
by Amazon